KU-885-005

Author's Introduction

Not one of these tales is true and all of them are. Each story in this collection hangs on incidents that occurred as I was growing up towards the end of the 1950s in Ashington, Northumberland, once known as the largest pit village in Europe. A few of the more public events even reached the pages of the *Ashington & District Advertiser*, the local newspaper of the time, and can still be found in the archives at Ashington Library. I have included some transcripts of the more interesting press articles in the section *Behind the Stories* at the back of this book.

One of the events I write about made headlines the world over and yet seems the most far-fetched; what storyteller would dare make up the extraordinary circumstances surrounding the tragic loss of the Busby Babes in the Munich air crash of 6 February 1958? A survivor of the crash, of course, was Ashington-born Bobby Charlton, only 20 years old at the time.

Well-chronicled facts are what they are and I have aimed to respect them. Throughout the stories, however, I have changed many details, for example the names of local characters. As they used to say every week in the TV programme *Dragnet*: "Only the names have been changed to protect the innocent." Well, that's part of my reason for creating new identities for the real people recollected here, but more than that I do so to signal the limits of autobiography in my writing. These stories are no more or less autobiographical than, say, Charles Dickens intended with *David Copperfield*, if I may be allowed the outrageous conceit of comparing my umble endeavour with one of the great works of English literature.

That is especially true when writing about family members. I am the sixth of seven Williams children whose lives were naturally intertwined in our early years. They will remember some of the events and catch shadowy glimpses of our relationships with each other and our parents. But the characters I have tried to shape in these stories are by no means reproductions of my real-life siblings.

Those readers familiar with Ashington will recognise many of the locations and features of the town, but they will also notice several apparent inaccuracies. If I have given a street a different name or appear to have moved a building to another place it's not a lapse of memory, honest. Often the change is for artistic purposes - poetic licence as the academics call it – but it's also a reminder that *WE NEVER HAD IT SO GOOD* is not meant to be taken for a historical work.

Yet so much of it is true, and I wonder if readers will be astonished as I was, recalling some of the things we did that we regarded as perfectly normal. Can you imagine now, for instance, sending a huge cardboard box filled with loose fireworks through the everyday post? That's what my uncle in Yorkshire did without a second thought when he wanted us to share some of his good fortune after a modest pools win in 1957. His kind gesture sparked off, in more ways than one, the episode described in the chapter *Uncle Barney's Box*.

Perhaps even more surprising is the latitude we had as children under the age of eleven to roam the streets at all hours. It's not as if my parents were particularly negligent – on the whole they made a reasonable go of the difficult job of raising seven children without much in the way of resources, and we've all turned out pretty decently, I think. (Nobody in prison at the time of writing.) I guess it was just that the perception of danger out there was so much less and children generally spent a lot more time outdoors than they do now. Mind you, if our folks knew what we were up to at times.

Something that struck me as I dredged my memory to recapture the behaviour and language was the casual, almost incidental cruelty of those days, from adult to child and between ourselves as children. I don't just mean the widespread use of corporal punishment in school and at home, but the way we categorised and referred to each other. Teachers and pupils alike talked blithely about children in the 'backward class'. We freely used nomenclatures such as 'Porky' and 'Smelly' as pet names for some of our peers. There were very few black people in Ashington at that time but if there had been it is likely they would often have heard terms like 'nigger' and 'darkie' used without shame. Political correctness had not been invented and stigmatisation, though common, was almost unconscious, even innocent in its ignorance. If in these stories I have occasionally made use of terms that would rightly be frowned on today it is because I wish to be authentic, not shocking.

One of the most difficult challenges in writing this book was finding an appropriate 'voice' for the central character. I wanted to show the reader that these stories are told by a man whose education and experiences have taken him away from the streets of Ashington, but I also wanted to reflect the thoughts and speech patterns of the boy as accurately and immediately as I was able, so I have tried to match the language to the moment. I hope any of my surviving former teachers will forgive the liberties taken with syntax and grammar in these pages. Please understand they represent my search for a voice that rings true in the narration and don't send this book back to me covered in red ink.

David Williams

REMEMBER, REMEMBER

Penny for the Guy

There used to be 19 working men's social clubs and 26 fish and chip shops in Ashington, Northumberland. Come out of any one of them any evening between Halloween and Bonfire Night and you'd be ambushed by a huddle of kids on hold-up duty around an ancient pram with a body inside. "Penny for the guy."

Looking at the kids around that pram and the grown-ups passing by or stopping for a moment to search for a little loose change in their pockets, you could easily be fooled into thinking they come from a time when the war's not been long finished. It's only the odd Teddy boy quiff or maybe a lass clicking along in white stilettos that brings things a bit more up to date. Those little lads hunching against the wind in their balaclavas could just as well be refugees with everything they've got in the world piled in an old pram, begging for bread instead of pennies. Of course the truth is they all have homes to go to, in the colliery rows maybe or the council estates, but they're marked out to be scuffing their heels against lamp-posts. Anyway they wouldn't be allowed to bring their friends home, not after dark, so they'll stay out as long as they dare.

One particular night me and Malcolm are raking the streets but not on the scrounge. There's just the two of us, sharing a tanner's worth of chips from Davison's. Cooke's is nearer but we've stopped going since our older brother Eddie broke off his engagement with their Joyce after he joined the Navy.

I say sharing but it's typical of Mal that he has to be the one who holds on to the packet. Kept his hands warm, he said. A few years later, when I passed my eleven–plus and went to the grammar school, I learned that possession is nine-tenths of the law. Right now I only knew that possession was nine-tenths of the chips.

"Penny for the guy?" some lad calls out from behind. We turn round and there's Billy Ridley trying to catch up. He's got no coat on, just an old woolly jumper three sizes too big. He's using one sleeve to smear snots away and the other sleeve's over the hand that's pulling the trolley-cart he's made for racing down Sheepwash Bank. Propped up in the cart is a sorry-looking guy that's so short of stuffing it looks as if it's been flattened by a steam-roller.

"Where you off?" says Malcolm, between chips.

"Grand Corner. The Evans's made twelve bob there last night."

"Hadaway."

"They did. I've just been in Rodway's wi' them, buying fireworks with the money."

"Well, *you'll* never get nowt," says Malcolm, kicking the back wheel of the cart. "Not with that guy. Here, put some more paper up its jacksy."

He scrunches up the chip wrappings into a parcel and lobs it into the cart. Then he puts his hand in his pocket. I panic for a second, thinking he's going to give Billy our change from the chips in that show-off way he has. But instead he pulls out the dabber stone we'd been using as a ball between our house and Davison's, and he toe-pokes it down the street.

"Howay youngun," he says to me. "Green doors this time. I'll gi' you three goals start."

And we chase after the dabber leaving Billy Ridley to stuff chip paper inside his scrawny guy.

"What you go and do that for?" Mal's complaining to me five minutes later. He's mad 'cause he's already scored in three green doors and we're only halfway home.

"I didn't mean it."

All I'd done was whack the dabber along the gutter and it had slipped down between the bars of a drain. It was the council's fault, not mine. They'd put the drain there.

"We'll just have to call it a draw," I say.

"You did that on purpose," moans Malcolm, striding ahead in the huff, hands deep in his pockets. I'm about to ask how he supposed the brother who couldn't hit a garage door had suddenly turned into Bobby Charlton when I see the menace round his shoulders and decide a distraction strategy is safer.

"Did you believe him?" I ask when we reach the corner of our street.

"Who?"

"Billy Ridley, about the Evans's making twelve shillin'."

"I dunno. Don't give a monkey's."

"Twelve bob, though."

I lay off for a minute, knowing I've said enough to get money spinning in Malcolm's brain. It's more than twice as much as we've got stashed in the tin under our bed for fireworks night. As we reach our gate I start up again.

"What do you reckon Billy'll get?"

"Nowt. Not with that flat-arsed dummy. I could make a better one mesel'."

It's a eureka moment. "Hey, why don't we?" I say, just as it comes into my head. "Why don't we make a guy and take it round the clubs? Bet we could cadge more than Billy Ridley."

"That's what I said, didn't I? It was my idea," says Mal, who'd never do anything his kid brother suggested until he'd thought of it first.

Back home is a shed next to the coalhouse that's jammed full of old junk and smells of cat's piss. It doesn't have a light so the first thing we have to do is sneak a candle and a box of matches from the scullery drawer.

Once, hiding from Dad's belt, I'd seen the wheels of a pushchair under a heap of stuff at the back of the shed. So while Mal spoaches around the house for clothes to dress the guy I have the job of shifting dried–up paint cans, dirty jam jars and Mam's old mangle to get at the buggy.

Making the guy turns out to be harder than we'd bargained for, especially having to work by candlelight. Mal has pinched more clothes than we need - shoving them out of our bedroom window while Mam's downstairs ironing and listening to the wireless - and we've found a stack of Ashington Advertisers in the shed to use as stuffing. The trouble is keeping all the bits of the dummy together.

Malcolm gets frustrated and starts kicking the body around the yard like a football.

"You're spoiling it. All the paper's coming out."

"Who cares? This guy's no flamin' good, is it? It's fallin' all over the place."

"Well, we just need some string or summat, join the different bits up."

"Some string or summat? Join the bits up? How the frig are you gonna do that, like?" Malcolm is world champion at scorn.

"I don't know. Just sort of sew it. With a big needle ... sort of thing."

I can't see Malcolm's face properly in the gloom but I know his sneer by heart.

"You dummy."

I half-flinch, expecting a kick, but it doesn't come. In fact nothing comes for about five seconds. No movement. No sound. It's the longest I've known my brother stay still unless he's asleep. Finally he speaks in a hushed tone, awed by his own genius.

"That's it," he says.

"What?"

"You can be the dummy."

"Eh?"

"It'll be great, man. We'll dress you up in all these clothes. Stick some paper inside. You'll be the best guy ever. We'll make a mint."

Once he has his heart set on something, Malcolm's not one for objections. In no time he has me nearly buried in the clothes he's thrown down. Most of it is stuff our Ed left behind so it's massive on me. I have to wear three layers of everything then Malcolm bulks it out with newspapers until I end up feeling like the Michelin Man.

He sits me down in the pushchair and lifts the candle to study his creation.

"Your head's the problem," he says, shaking his.

Next thing he's hunting around the shed with the candle, I'm worrying he might be after a saw. In a minute he comes out riving at the remains of a Frido ball, one we'd sacrificed under the wheels of a coal train in the summer holidays. He tears a long split in the skin of the ball.

"Try this for size," he goes. I can still feel how the edges scraped my ears as he rammed the burst ball over my head, and the smell of the damp plastic inside.

"Perfect," I hear him say. "Just needs a scarf round and a bit paint for the face."

"I can't see anything."

"You don't have to."

"I can't breathe properly."

"Stop moanin'. You'll get to take it off when there's nobody about."

Half an hour later, my backside sore from Malcolm charging at kerbs and sweat dripping inside my Frido head, we're parked outside the Comrades, Ashington's busiest working men's club. It's already after ten so most of the other kids have been hauled back home, leaving the coast clear for us. Our dad's on night shift so it'll just be the hairbrush not the belt when we get in. Supposing we get ten bob or more it'll be worth it, and there's plenty blokes going in and out of the club at this time. All the signs are good.

The rule is that every time Mal yells out "Penny for the guy" I have to hold my breath and play dead in the buggy. He's brought a jam jar from the shed and I can hear the regular clink of change dropping onto glass. It's what keeps me from dying for real as the night goes on. That and comments from folk who bend over the pushchair as if they're admiring a new baby.

"Mind, it's a smart guy, that. Well made."

"He looks a bit like wor gaffer."

"Canny. You'd win a prize with that one, son."

Between customers our Malcolm sometimes remembers and sometimes forgets to sneak open the split edges of the ball to let me suck some air in. Now and again he'll hiss a secret message from the side of his mouth but I can never make out the words so I concentrate on staying as still as I can and trying to blot out all the itches and cramps working at me underneath. After what seems like hours he crouches on his honkers and whispers, "How you doing in there?"

"I've got pins and needles and I'm dyin' for a slash. Are we not finished yet?"

"Just about. I'm thinkin' we'll go back the long way round, past the Arcade. It'll be chuckin' out time at the dance."

I'm relieved when the kerb charging and pavement bumping start again so at least I can get some circulation going. Once we reach the Arcade the people passing by sound different. The voices are younger, more like our Eddie's age, and they're a lot noisier tripping out the dance hall than the ones from the Comrades. There's lasses giggling in groups and lads calling out at each other in harsh voices that sound put on, as if they're all practising for the part of tough guy.

Mal keeps hustling for pennies but there's not much going in the jar now, even though there's more people round the buggy than before. It's getting shoved and joggled so much I'm finding it hard to stay still. I want the toilet and I want to go home.

Then I hear this bloke. I can even smell the drink on him and I can tell he's leaning right over the pushchair with his legs apart trying to keep his balance like our dad does when he's been on the hoy.

"What's this, sonny?" he asks as if he's being friendly but my brother and me both know the signals well enough.

"It's a guy, what does it look like?" comes our Malcolm who's got a lot more guts than I have, to be honest.

"That's not a guy, it's a friggin' freak o' nature. It's a friggin' freak, this," he says louder, showing off to his audience. "A friggin' joke. He's got a ball for a heed."

"Got more brains than you, Varty," somebody shouts and gets a laugh.

Varty's niggled and cuts back in straight away. "He wants puttin' down, that's what."

I can feel a chill in the air from his threat. He takes a step away from the buggy but I get a sense from the crowd that he's not finished. I hear our Malcolm say, "Leave him alone," then more urgent, frightened. "Leave off him, he's real!"

Next thing there's this huge smack into my chest and a stabbing pain. I give out a massive yell and hurl myself out the buggy, knocking it over. Varty screams like a girl and there's all sorts of commotion and running. I fall forward onto my knees, gasping, and there's something wet trickling down, spreading underneath me.

Mal grabs me and rips the Frido off my head. I can see people in the background until Mal blots them out with his scared face.

"Are you all right, kid? Are you all right?"

"Ah, Mal, I've gone and pissed me pants."

It was a knife Varty pulled on us that night. Just a pocket knife but with the force he used it could have killed me if it wasn't for all the layers of clothes and newspapers. All these years later if my skin's cold you can still see a thin white scar where the blade went through to the breastbone.

Naturally we say nowt about this when Mam catches us trying to sneak back into the house. She brays us both with her hairbrush. A month later Malcolm gets a second skelping when our Ed comes home from the Navy to find a hole in the front of his best dress shirt. He hasn't a clue what really happened, but he reckons he knows who to blame.

Mal thought it was all worthwhile, though. He can still make us both laugh till we cry when he talks about the shock that tosser Varty got, the night Guy Fawkes jumped up at him.

And we can still both tell you the exact amount we counted out of the jam jar when we emptied it onto our bedspread around midnight. Twenty six shillings and fourpence. That bought a hell of a lot of fireworks in 1958.

Old Man Tate

On Wagon Train, a telly programme I used to watch, the white folks travelling west always made their camp in a square to protect themselves against Red Indians. At the back of our street in Ashington was a square of cottages where old folks were always on their guard against young savages like us from the council estate.

In the middle of the square was a green that the council looked after. We thought it was wasted on the old people. It was flat and neat, just about perfect for a game of football or cricket. But we couldn't step on the green without a window opening and some cracked voice yelling, "Get out of it! Go play round your own doors!"

The only fun we could get in the square was daring each other to run through the arch that was the way in then dash right round the pathways and out again before anybody caught us. The one to watch for most was Mr Tate from number eleven. Did you ever hear that story about the troll who hid under a bridge and stopped goats getting into his field to eat grass? Old Man Tate was like the troll, always on the lookout. He had the gruffest, scariest voice and a walking stick that he would sometimes poke out as we pelted past his door.

Funny, though, we were kind of fascinated by Old Man Tate. If we maybe saw him walking along the road we'd start to follow him for no reason. Our Malcolm and Derek Nesbitt from along the doors would copy him, making on they had a stick and a stiff leg going sideways, more like

Charlie Chaplin really. Or they'd give him the fingers behind his back. Mostly, I just followed.

Mam told us that Mr Tate didn't only have a limp – he had a wooden leg. She reckoned he'd had his real leg blown off in the First World War. I thought a lot about that. I wondered how much it had hurt, how he stopped the bleeding and what happened to the leg after it got blown off.

We had our own war games once the nights were cutting in and fireworks went on sale at Rodway's, the corner shop that never closed. Bangers were a penny each. We'd all get half a dozen and some loose matches to strike on the walls or the road. They became hand grenades that we lobbed at each other from hiding places in bin corners, back yards and on coalhouse roofs.

The trick was not to let go until the fuse was nearly burnt through and sparks were spitting out, so the enemy had less time to move away when the banger landed next to him. Get it wrong and the banger went off in your hand.

That happened to me a couple of times. It felt the same as getting the belt – stinging and throbbing, like sharp pins inside trying to burst through your skin. I'd heard about kids getting fingers blown off by messing about with fireworks but I suppose we were just lucky.

We're playing Jerries against the English with bangers one night when Old Man Tate suddenly bursts on the scene.

"Stop that flamin' racket!" he yells. "Had yoursel's away."

Nez had a right gob on him and always answered back.

"Hadaway yoursel'," he shouts. "We're not doing nowt to you."

Tate lifts his stick in a rage and we're gone, streaking through the cut like cats when somebody rattles a bin lid.

We regroup, squatting under the lamp-post next to Derek Nesbitt's house.

"I'm pig sick o' that bloke," says Nez. "He's got no right to tell us what to do. He's not me dad."

"Or your granda'," I put in. Nez just gives one of his looks and I clam up.

"He wants shutting in his box," says Mal. I think he means Mr Tate, not me. "You should set your Towser on him. You should train him to chase after his stick."

Nez stands up. "I've got a better idea," he says. "I'm gonna put the wind right up his jacksy."

"What you gonna do, like?"

"You'll see. Howay."

A few minutes later me and Mal are staring through the arch into Bolam Square, watching Derek Nesbitt creep along in the dark to Mr Tate's door. My heart's racing and I've got a sick feeling in my guts. I don't know what Nez is up to, and it's not as if we have any rules or anything, but I can sense this is summat we wouldn't normally get involved in. It's wrong.

My brother must feel the same 'cause when Nez reaches the front door Mal grips me by the shoulder. And when Nez takes a banger out of his pocket and strikes a match on Tate's step Malcolm tugs at my jumper as if I was Nez and whispers, "No, come away."

But he doesn't come away. He puts the match to the fuse and we can see it glowing. Then it disappears through Tate's letterbox and Nez starts sprinting back to us. Mal and me are statues for a second, then we hear a dull bang and we're off, running for our lives towards the street lights on the other side of the estate.

For days afterwards I jump every time I hear a knock at the door, expecting Old Man Tate or even the police to be on our doorstep. But that knock never comes. Which worries me even more 'cause now I'm wondering what might have happened to Mr Tate.

We've steered clear of Bolam Square since the night Nez set off his banger, but the morning after Guy Fawkes I start spying from a distance while I make on to be looking around for burnt-out rockets and such like. There's no sign of Mr Tate, either outside his place or on the road to the shops.

In the afternoon I come closer till I'm right up to the archway. As far as I can see from there his curtains look to be drawn. I know one way of getting him to come out, but I'm scared to do it. My heart's beating like it was that other night, then suddenly I'm galloping along the paths around the square, scuffing my feet deliberately to make a noise. I even try to shout "Geronimo!" as I turn the corners but I say it more to myself, not really yelling it out. A couple of nets twitch at windows, but nothing from number eleven.

Back at the archway I'm panicking. What if he had a heart attack when the banger exploded? What if it set a blaze away and he's died trying to put it out?

I walk on jelly legs to his house, at the same time shoving my hands in my pockets, trying to act like I go and see Mr Tate every day. I tap quietly on the door, then a little bit louder but there's no answer. I kneel down and push open the letterbox, looking and sniffing for signs of fire. Nothing.

Our Ed once told us that when a body's been lying dead for days it makes maggots and they turn into flies. I sidle along the wall with pebbledash scraping my cheek to look for flies behind the glass. There's an ashtray, a couple of drawing pins and the back of a photo frame on the window sill, but no flies and nothing else I can see past the curtain.

I turn to check if any of the neighbours are watching and get such a fright the back of my head hits the window. Mr Tate's standing inches away, his hand gripped white on his stick. His eyes are like a killer's.

"What you think you're doing, you little toe-rag? After burgling us now, is it?"

He reaches out to grab my arm but I manage to wriggle away and run off along the path. He shouts from behind, "You'll not get away. I know where you live."

That night I wake in a sweat from a dream where Old Man Tate was holed up in our shed, throwing hand grenades that turned into giant bluebottles splatting against my bedroom window.

Next morning I nick half a crown out of my mam's purse, just in case. If Mr Tate comes round to ours I'm planning to leave home, get on a bus going to the country and live in some woods until they're all sorry I'm gone.

At school two lads from Malcolm's class come round with a tray of poppies and a collecting tin. The teacher makes a speech about war heroes and these bigger lads parade up and down the rows with the tray. Most kids have pennies or threepences they've brought to drop in the tin. I put my half crown in and take a poppy.

I go straight from school and knock on Mr Tate's door. I'm wishing I could be carrying a white flag. Mr Tate opens the door and stands looking down at me, saying nowt. I can see a singe on his door mat and wonder if it was from the banger. Then I say, "I brought you a poppy."

"Where's your tin? You haven't got a tin."

"I'm not collecting. I bought it for you as a present," says I, lifting the poppy up to him. "For being a war hero."

He takes it. "I was never in the war," he says.

"I mean the First World War. When you lost your leg."

"I didn't lose me leg in the war. I was never in the Great War neither."

I don't know what else to say. We both just stand for a while. Then he says, "Do you know where the flower park is?"

"Yes, sir. Over at the Hirst."

"Get across there and have a look at the statue next to the side gate. Go and learn yoursel' some history."

He puts his poppy in his buttonhole and stands at the door watching as I walk back through the archway.

I knew the statue he meant. You were supposed to be able to get a drink from some taps underneath it but somebody had blocked them up with little red pebbles.

I go across to have a look. The statue is a pitman wearing his work clothes and a flat cap. He doesn't have a pick or anything but he's holding a miner's lamp right up to his eyes. On the stand is a picture of a pit in a metal plate and on the other side another metal plate that tells you who paid for the statue and what it was for.

It says: 'In memory of their fellow workmen who lost their lives in the Woodhorn Colliery explosion on Sunday, August 13th 1916.' There's a list of thirteen names underneath.

I sit on a park bench for a minute, thinking about Mr Tate down the pit with his leg blown away waiting for somebody to come and find him among all those dead bodies. Then it turns cold and I walk home.

Old Man Tate never did come round to our house and I never went back to his. I passed him a few times going to the shops and he would give a little wink if I was on my own, like we were sharing a secret. Then I stopped seeing him altogether.

"Ah look, that Mr Tate's died, from the cottages," Mam says to my dad one day when she's flicking through the Ashington Advertiser. "Him what lost his leg in the war."

My dad just nods and pokes at the coals in the fireplace.

The Black Monk

I'd say the only scary thing about Halloween was sneaking across the fence at Duggie's farm to snag turnips for lanterns. The rest of it was kids' stuff, really. Younger kids than us, I mean, trailing lighted bagies along their street on the end of a string or parking them on the step to warn off the witches. There wasn't any trick-or-treating then – I think that came in later from America – so there wasn't much to do once you'd hollowed out your turnip and stuck the candle in.

Still, we always left home feeling that we'd come across something spooky. The pools of light under the far lamp-posts seemed to expect it. Past the glow of our lanterns the shadows seemed deeper and it was like somebody inside the dark was watching us. But nowt ever happened. Not even on the night Dennis Freeman warned me off crossing People's Park. It was what came after that was weird.

It's maybe about ten o'clock Halloween night by the time we're passing the gates outside the park. We'd sat in our camp down the dene until the lanterns petered out, then we left them on the railway line for the coal wagons to squash. Since then we've been wandering halfway round Ashington, just on the mooch, disappointed, and now we're on our way home.

"Howay, Dennis," I say. "Let's cut through the park."

"No, don't," from Dennis, pulling my arm back as I'm opening the gate.

"What's up, like?"

"The Black Monk'll get ya."

"Eh?"

"You know the old bandstand?" he goes on, dropping his voice. "The one with the shutters round it?"

"Yeah."

"There's summat lives in there called the Black Monk. And at night, when people walk through the park, he follows them. They can't see him 'cause he's all in black with this like black monk's hood on."

"How does anybody know about him, then?" I want to show Dennis I'm not that daft. "Anyway, how can he get out of the bandstand when it's all boarded up?"

"There's a door underneath and some steps." Dennis pulls himself up to the railings and peers through them as if he's peering inside a cage. "Go and have a look if you don't believe us. I wouldn't go now, though, if I were you. It's safe in the daytime. You'll not see him then. And you'll not see him at night neither, until you turn round."

"Why would you turn round?"

Instead of answering straight away Dennis jumps off the railings and starts doing an impression of a zombie, dragging his feet through the dry leaves that have fallen from the trees in People's Park.

"What you doing?"

"Hear them leaves?" he says. "Suppose you're walking through the park and you hear a noise like that, behind ya."

"It might just be an echo though, mightn't it? It might just be me walking through the leaves and hearing an echo... sort o' thing."

"But say you stopped and you can still hear it. Only it's getting nearer."

"I wouldn't turn round."

"You'd have to. He like makes you do it. And when you turn round...slash."

Dennis turns and claws at my face like he's a wild cat.

"Shit!" I jump back, nearly run off, then stop. It's only Dennis. He looks at his own hand, with his fingers all spread out, then he looks up at me.

"There was this lass," he says. "Got her eye half torn out and scratches this deep all down her cheek. She went to the hospital and you know what they found stuck in her face?"

"No."

"A huge fish hook." Dennis spreads his hand out again and I watch, fascinated. "That's the thing about this Black Monk. He has massive fish hooks on the ends of all his fingers. He follows ya till you turn round, then slash, he's got ya."

"Where did you hear all this?"

"Obvious, innit? Where does me mam work? They've had to hush it up so they don't panic everybody. She told me on the quiet. But you're not to say nothing to nobody, right? Top secret."

Dennis's mam works at Ashington Hospital. So the story must be true.

"Do you still want to go through the park?" he asks.

We take the long way round instead and to be honest with you I've never been so glad to get back in the house.

Of course I don't intend to tell my brother, but when the Black Monk slashes at me in the middle of the night I cry out in my sleep, rousing Malcolm. Born nosy, he shakes me awake, demanding to know what I'm dreaming about.

"Nothing. Just football an' that."

"Was it nick about football. It was a nightmare. You were yellin' and squirmin'. You've still got a sweat on." He gets me in a half nelson. "Howay, spit it out."

"Get off, will ya? It was just about the Black Monk."

"The who?"

So of course I have to tell him the story before he breaks my arm, even though Dennis warned me not to. When I'm finished I can tell he's impressed but he doesn't want to admit it's true straight away since it wasn't him telling it.

"We'll just have to go and have a look at this bandstand, see what's what," he says after a bit.

"Not at night-time, though."

"Naturally not at night-time. We won't be able to see much in the dark, will we? Dope." And he flicks the side of my head hard with his middle finger in that way he does.

The next day's Sunday so the two of us and Derek Nesbitt, who Mal's told, run across to People's Park before dinner. We must have seen that bandstand dozens of times before but we gawp at it as if Dan Dare's just landed it in the park with an alien inside. Only instead of being a shiny new spaceship it's this drab wooden affair with paint peeling off the boards that have been used to shut the place up.

"There's the door, see," says Mal as if it was him told us all about it in the first place.

Sure enough under the ridge of the platform is a dirty green door hardly bigger than a coal hatch with some steps leading down to it from our level.

I point to the padlock on the door. "He couldn't get out though, could he?"

"Ah, that's where you're wrong, but," comes Nez. "I saw this picture once where some Jews or summat were hiding from the Gestapo and there was a padlock on their door to make on it was locked. Except there was secret hinges on the same side as the padlock so when they wanted to get out at night for food they opened a bolt on the other side of the door and got out that way."

We all peer at the door but it's covered with old paint and dirt so we can't tell whether it's a trick door or not. Not from the distance we're keeping away, and nobody's volunteering to go down for a closer look.

"Aggh, there's nobody inside," says Mal at last.

He picks a muckle stone up from the grass and chucks it at the bandstand. The stone booms off one of the boards.

Nez is up like a rabbit. "Christ! Did you hear that?"

"What?"

"Like a roar. Did you not hear the roar? There's somebody in there!"

And we're away like the clappers, scattering leaves all the way to the park gates, bursting our lungs till we reach the safety of our own streets.

It's cold in bed that night and I grip my toes in my hands, tucking my knees up to my chin, but even while I'm shivering I can feel a clamminess around my shoulders that I've got from worrying about the Black Monk. I know Malcolm's thinking about him as well. He only lies stiff on his back like that when he can't get himself off to sleep. I feel as if we're both listening out for something. When a coal train goes by in the night I'm listening so hard I can follow it for miles before it finally fades away and leaves a space for another sound that never quite comes but is there, waiting on the far side of the railway line.

I don't know how it happens but by Monday playtime the whole school is talking about the Black Monk. I keep out of Dennis Freeman's way as I know he'll blame me, but I reckon somebody from the hospital's been blabbing 'cause there's stuff going round that's news to me. Like the Black Monk puts the sign of the cross on your cheek same as Zorro does with his Z. Like somebody saw his face under the hood once and it was covered in horrible scars so he probably does this for revenge and he's maybe not a real monk but he just wears the hood to hide his scars.

Tell you what, I've never seen so many lasses coming up to the fence that separates our yard from theirs to talk to the lads on the other side. Usually they're away doing bays or skippie or some other lasses' games, but now it seems they cannot get enough of hearing about the Black Monk.

Wednesday afternoon another weird thing happens. At the end of the day Mr Carrick makes every class go and sit on the floor in the hall. He strides to the front as if he's going to do an assembly, then *he* starts on about the Black Monk.

"I understand that some silly rumour has been circulating the playground in my school," he says. "And I'm here to tell you that this stupid talk is going to cease as of this moment."

He stands for ages and looks down at us with these cruel eyes like he's trying to stare us all out or turn us to stone. Then he goes on.

"I do not intend to give false credit to this story by repeating it now. Suffice it to say there is *nothing* to fear in People's Park. The one thing you need to fear is my strap which will come down hard on *any* boy whom I hear or have reported to me as repeating this foolish lie. Do I make myself perfectly plain?"

"Yes, sir," from all of us in chorus.

"Dismissed."

Once we're far enough away from the school to be sure Carrick and his spies aren't listening in, we go over the whole thing again. Suddenly, Nez snaps his fingers.

"That proves it," he says. "It's a cover-up."

"Eh?"

"Think about it, right. No kid in the school is going to tell old Carrick about the Black Monk. So how's he know about it? From another grown-up, prob'ly somebody at the hospital. They've asked him to help keep it hushed up, so he's trying to stop us talking to each other."

"And he's making on it's all made up," adds Mal. "Double bluff, sort o' thing. That's what I was thinking all along."

I'm not sure what I'm thinking by now, but by the time the local paper comes on Friday we're all convinced about the Black Monk 'cause it's there in black and white, front page.

Terrified Teenagers Flee from Park

The story's about this young couple eating chips in People's Park shelter on Tuesday night and the lass looks out and sees a black shape coming towards them from behind the bandstand. They know straight away it's the Black Monk and they run to the gates but they hear him chasing after them. The girl says he was that close she could hear him panting, and they reached the gates just in time. He didn't try to follow them outside the park so they got away.

The rest of the story is about the police and the council saying that maybe the couple made a mistake with it being dark but how they're keeping an open mind and going to look into it.

Anyway it's obviously not top secret any more, so when I go and seek Dennis on Friday night I'm not bothered about mentioning it to his mam while he's away putting his shoes on.

"Have you had any more of them Black Monk cases at the hospital, Mrs Freeman?"

"What?"

"You know, like that lass who got her eye tore out with the fish hook. The one you nursed."

"I'm not a nurse, just do cleaning there three days a week. I haven't got a clue what you're on about."

"Oh, it was only your Dennis said..."

"Hey, what stories have you been making up about me being a nurse at the hospital?" she says to Dennis as he comes back into the kitchen.

"I never said you was a nurse."

"And what's this about a Black Monk?"

"Oh, nowt, Mam, just a joke. Like a Halloween story, sort o' thing. I'll not be late, right."

And he shoves us out of the back door smartish and up the lane before his mam can say anything else.

I never mention this to Mal or Derek Nesbitt. On Saturday morning the three of us go up to People's Park for a spoach about. Just inside the entrance there's a little hunchback bloke sweeping leaves off the path. Next to him there's a two-wheeled contraption he's using to pull along his tools and a couple of bins. The hunchback has to stretch to lift the leaves into one of the bins and he practically disappears when he reaches in to flatten them down. Nez reckons there's summat queer going on 'cause he's never seen a parkie working here on a Saturday.

Further in there's a couple of council workmen taking the shutters off the bandstand. They've attracted quite a little crowd of folk watching, even though there's not much to see but a mess of pigeon shit on the deck where the bands used to play. The little door's open below and every so often the workmen go through to stash the boards under the platform. There's a policeman, a special, keeping an eye on things in the park.

"They've must've caught him at last," says Malcolm.

Nez wonders where they'll put the Black Monk away. "The loony bin in Morpeth, d'ya reckon?"

"Nah, he's too dangerous for there," comes Mal. "He'll be in a straitjacket in Durham Jail. Prob'ly for the rest of his life."

And we move off for a turn on the teapot lid, confident that Ashington People's Park is a safe place again.

Hot Dogs

"**M**y God, we're turning just like America."That's
from Mam as the bus we're on passes the
Grand Corner one Friday night. It's a ride
that sticks in my mind. Why? Well, number one, just
her and me travelling anywhere together practically
never happens. Number two, though Ashington's
quite big I'm used to walking or running from one
place to another – we only take the bus for going to
the Miners' Picnic in Bedlington or the odd day to
Morpeth. Three, getting to ride upstairs. Four, what
we see at the Grand Corner that makes Mam think
we're turning into Yanks.

The reason we're on the bus is we've been across to
Auntie Emily's in Woodhorn Road with a bag full of
Malcolm's old clothes for taking up. He's grown out of
them but I haven't properly grown into them, so that's
where Auntie Emily and her sewing machine come in. We
walked there holding the bag between us but Mam was
jiggered by the finish so Auntie Emily persuaded her to
take the bus back. Riding on the top deck is my present
for hours of standing still while Auntie Emily crawled
round me with pins in her mouth.

And that's how we happen to see Marco's hot
dog stand on its very first night in Ashington. The
bus has to wait at the crossing so we get a good
look. There's a lot of folk on the pavement, mainly
lads and lasses on their way to the pictures. Some's
crowding round the stall, some's stuffing their

faces with hot dogs, and loads are just hanging about watching what's going on. It's like a party.

The stand's a queer affair. It's sort of a silver metal box on a bike, or rather a trike since there's a wheel either side of the box and one at the back with a saddle. As the bus pulls away I see that the bloke dishing out the hot dogs is from the shop next door to the Pavilion.

"That's Marco from the Piv ice cream shop, Mam. He's Italian, not American."

"Same difference," says Mam, counting her change for the conductor. "Look at Frank Sinatra. He's Mafia an' all, they reckon."

I haven't a clue what she's on about, so I shut up.

At this time I've never eaten a hot dog but I've seen Kookie and his girlfriend sharing one on 77 Sunset Strip. All the teenage lads wanted to be like Kookie and when Malcolm and me go up to the Grand Corner on Saturday night to look at the hot dog stand we see plenty of lads leaning against the barriers combing their hair back and dangling their fags out their mouths, looking the lasses up and down. Nobody has a sports car though, or any sort of car. Andy Clough's brought along his racer, pretty cool I'm thinking, but even I know he should have taken off his bike clips.

"Ha' you packed in your ice cream shop, Marco?" pipes up Mal. We know him a bit from buying sweets on the way to the matinée at the Piv.

"Ah, no. Ice creams in the day, hot dogs at night-time. That's the future for Marco. Hey, you boys wanna make some pocket money tonight?"

He doesn't need to ask twice, we're round him like puppies to hear what we've got to do. Marco puts down his tongs and prods below his belt with his fingers.

"I got a hernia, man. Riding this heavy trike's doing me no good. I need somebody to take it back to the yard when I've finished. I give you a bob and a free hot dog. Good deal?"

It's a great deal as long as we can smuggle our way out the house to get back to the Grand Corner for eleven when Marco stops selling for the night. We've got a trick, though, that's worked for us before. After we go to bed we stuff our bolster and pillows under the sheets to make it look as if we're both lying asleep, then we put our clothes back on and nip out of the bedroom window onto the shelter and down the drainpipe.

I'm not surprised Marco doesn't want to pedal his stall back, since it turns out to be bloody hard work. There's a couple of gas bottles under the fryer as well as all the stock and the water inside.

It's not so bad when you get it going but it's a bugger to steer and if you change direction too quick or bump a kerb the stuff sloshes out. I nearly tip the whole caboodle over when I hit a dustbin somebody's been using for goals back of Maple Street. Trouble is there's no lights on the bike.

Mal and me take turns and we more or less get the hang of it by the time we reach the yard behind Marco's shop. It's worth it anyway, not just for the shilling but for the massive hot dogs Marco gives us both before we set away.

"Anything on top?" he asks, and I go for tomato sauce.

Malcolm's nosing along the shelf. "What's that yellow stuff?"

"Mustard."

"I'll try it."

Marco looks doubtful. "Sure?" and Mal nods so he squeezes a yellow line the whole length of the sausage and hands it over.

I take my first ever bite of hot dog and look across to share this special moment with my brother. Malcolm's eyes are watering and his mouth, crammed with bread roll, is wide open, gasping for air.

"Good?" Marco asks.

"Fantastic," says I.

"Whooar!" from Mal.

Anyway, Marco's pleased with the job we do and makes another deal with us. We end up taking the trike to and from the Grand Corner every Thursday, Friday and Saturday for five bob all in and hot dogs every night, no mustard. By the second week he trusts us so much he just leaves the stall when he's finished and we pick it up, helping ourselves to hot dogs as we go.

On the fourth Thursday we set up the stall as usual and run home. Dad's on fore shift this week, having to traipse off to pit in the early hours, so he's in a bad fettle. We go to bed sharpish to keep out of his way.

By quarter to eleven Malcolm's arranging the pillows under the sheets ready for the off. I'm first out of the window onto the shelter. I'm just reaching for the drainpipe when the back door opens and Dad comes out with a scuttle and shovel. I freeze.

Dad's got his back to me, opening the coalhouse door. I turn in slow motion and slink face down onto the shelter as he starts to fill the scuttle. I might get away with this. Then Mal drops out of the window and lands on my arse.

"Oww!"

"What you doing down there, you stupid...?"

Dad turns his head and Malcolm spots him for the first time.

"Shit!" he says, under his breath.

"What the hell's going on?" Dad yells up.

"We're just playing, Dad," says I, weakly.

"I'll play you, you little monkeys." And he storms into the house.

Mal and I climb quickly back through the window and sort the bed out before he gets up the stairs. By the time the bedroom door opens our heads are side by side on the pillows, though we've still got our clothes on underneath. Dad undoes his belt buckle and we pull the blankets tight around us.

Later, when the sneck of the gate lets us know that he's away to work, we dare to speak again.

"Don't know what you're snivelling at," says Mal. "He hardly touched you. I got the buckle end."

"Not snivelling, just got a runny nose."

Mal hauls himself up to look out the window. "What time is it?"

"After twelve."

"No point in going now. Anyway, *she'll* be poking her head round the door next."

"What about Marco's trike?"

"He'll have seen it's not in the yard. He'll go back and fetch it."

Mal flops down onto his pillow. "That's knacked it for us," he says.

And we both lie there in the dark thinking about the five bobs and hot dogs we're going to miss.

In the school yard next morning we're playing squashy-in-the-corner when there's a commotion at the top end. Boys are running to join the big circle that normally means one thing.

"Fight!" shouts Mal. "Howay." And we run up to see who's possing who. Except it's not a fight. When we push through the crowd there's Melvin Dodds from the backward class standing behind Marco's stall with tongs in his hand. He's never had so much attention and he's got a huge grin on his face as he dishes out hot dogs to all and sundry.

"Hey, Smelly, this is cold," some kid shouts. He always gets Smelly, not Melvin.

"Hoi us a sausage," another lad calls out. Everybody's laughing and pushing each other, wound up by the insane sight of Marco's hot dog stall in our playground. And Smelly's in the middle, loving it. Then the whistle goes.

First whistle we're supposed to stop and freeze, whatever we're doing. Second whistle we're meant to run into our class lines ready for marching in. This time we stand stock still after the first blast, but after that it's silence.

Then the circle parts like it's been prised open and Mr Carrick is stood there, fists on his hips and a right face on him, whistle in one hand, his leather strap in the other. It's High Noon and Melvin Dodds is a dead man.

Only Smelly thinks it's Keystone Cops time. He hurls a hot dog at the teacher and before old Carrick can get over the shock he's up on the saddle and pedalling the trike through the crowd to the other end of the yard. A few kids give the seat a shove to help him along and soon he's got steam up, with Carrick chasing after him blowing his whistle and all of us acting like extras, whooping and cheering on the sidelines.

When Smelly reaches the toilet block he tries to wheel round so he doesn't get trapped at the bottom end of the yard. But he's travelling too fast and Marco's trike tips up, ditching Smelly and splattering stuff across the playground. Before Carrick can catch him Smelly's up on his feet again. He stands on the metal container and jumps up from there to reach the roof of the toilets.

Carrick comes to a stop in the middle of a mess of sausages, onions and water.

"I'll have your guts for garters, laddie," he shouts up at Melvin Dodds.

Smelly stands with his legs apart on top of the flat roof, gives Carrick a double V sign, then escapes over the other side of the toilet block. We can't help ourselves – we all just burst out clapping.

"Get into your lines!" yells Carrick, and we do as we're told but we all know he'll never get back what Smelly's taken away from him.

Marco got his hot dog trike returned with a few dents in it, but he seemed to lose interest after that. He had a new business idea instead. When Mal and me finally pluck up the courage to go into his shop one Saturday before the matinée we find him stacking records in a brand new jukebox.

"How do you like my new coffee bar, boys?" he says, so pleased with himself he doesn't even mention our leaving his trike to get nicked by Melvin Dodds. As well as the jukebox he's made room for a couple of Formica tables and he's fixed up an espresso machine behind the ice cream counter.

"What do you like? Tommy Steele? Cliff Richard?"

We choose Wake Up Little Susie by The Everly Brothers and while the record's playing we mime it for Marco, using strawberry Mivvis for microphones. He laughs so much he forgets to charge us for the lollies. Or maybe he's just letting us know that everything's OK.

Uncle Barney's Box

My least favourite firework of all time was Golden Rain. The most frustrating was the Catherine Wheel. The best was what we called the Jumpy Jack.

The Golden Rain was just a tiny tube you stuck in the ground. When you put a match to it all that happened was a feeble shower of sparks would come out about six inches high. You kept expecting it to do summat else, but it never did. This shower just went on and on then fizzled out.

When we were buying fireworks we'd never pick Golden Rain or Silver Fountain which was the same thing only with different colour sparks. But they'd always be in those two and sixpenny boxes you could get that were already made up.

We'd never buy *them*. Apart from the measly fireworks inside they generally had pictures on the box of posh-looking kids with school caps and ties looking all rosy-cheeked and having a jolly good time. They must have been easy pleased. Some of the boxes even said 'No bangers' like it was a recommendation. Nobody in their right mind would buy a box of fireworks that didn't have bangers. Not that we generally bought our fireworks in a box.

We usually got ours from Rodway's or Moore's where they were loose and you could pick what you wanted. Anyway we hardly ever had as much as half a dollar at one time so we bought just a few pennies' worth here and there to keep under the bed ready for bonfire night. Except for bangers of course, which we set off whenever we could.

We loved rockets, Roman Candles, Aerial Bombs and Jumpy Jacks. We always bought a couple of Catherine Wheels hoping at least one would work properly when we pinned it to the clothes prop, lit it and gave it a turn to start it off. There was nowt better than a Catherine Wheel whizzing round with colours changing and sparks whooshing out the tail, but mostly they either hung without spinning while the sparks fizzed onto the ground or they dropped off the clothes prop altogether and burned out in the weeds.

Jumpy Jacks, though, were fantastic. They were stubby and squiggly. You lit the fuse at one end and every few seconds the fizzer would bang and jump all over the place. You never knew where it was going so you could never really get out of the way of it. The best fireworks are ones that scare you and ones where you don't know what's going to happen next. That's why Jumpy Jacks were great.

The best Bonfire Night we ever had was when Uncle Barney from Yorkshire won the pools. It wasn't a fortune, not like that Viv Nicholson woman a couple of years later who said she was going to spend, spend, spend and finished up in the Sunday papers. I suppose his win was less than a hundred pounds but we didn't know a thing about it until this huge parcel arrived.

As far as I can remember we'd never had a parcel through the post before, not even Mam and Dad. Never a parcel and never a telegram. And this one's not even addressed to them, it's addressed to me and Malcolm and our little sister Jeannie.

We rip the paper off like it's Christmas and find a big cardboard box underneath with 'Fairy Snow' and the words 'whiteness plus mildness' half covered over with brown tape. Mal cuts through the tape with his pocket knife and opens up the box.

There's a note from Uncle Barney but we hardly notice it. We're busy drooling over the best stash of fireworks we've ever set our eyes on. Spangled Star Bombs, Traffic Lights, Spaceships, Mount Vesuvius, Screamers, Jack in the Box... There are bigger rockets and Roman Candles than we could ever afford, a Triangle Wheel and a Mine of Serpents you'd need two hands to carry. Plenty of bangers and Jumpy Jacks. But no Golden Rains. Uncle Barney knew how to buy fireworks.

Of course with fireworks like these we have to build a bonfire to match. Our house might be too little for everybody who has to live in it, but one thing we can crow about is a massive back garden, full of weeds. We always have the biggest bonfire in the street, and these are days when just about every clan in Ashington has their own bonfire. You can keep your big, safe public displays that come in years later, where you can't get anywhere near the action unless you're well in with the Round Table or some such. What's the use of fireworks if you can't let them off yourself?

The only bonfire to beat ours for size is the Bywell Road gang's. Their houses back onto a scruffy swing park where the whole gang gets together to build one big bonfire on some rough ground that's supposed to be a kick-about area.

They start on it just after Halloween night, pulling the long planks off the fences by the railway line and leaning them together like a wigwam to make the centre of their bonfire. Over the next few days all sorts of rubbish comes out to stack around the planks – bust-up settees, mattresses, cardboard boxes, tatty carpets – and same as us they wander down the dene to find dead wood, though we reckon they snap big branches off healthy trees as well, judging by all the smoke their bonfire gives out every year.

It's Malcolm's idea to do a raid. "Why not?" he says. "They'll not miss a few planks and a couple o' chairs."

"What's the point? We've got our own stuff," I argue, always the anxious one. "Anyway, they'll have theirs guarded."

"It's a special year, that's why, what with Uncle Barney's fireworks. You've got to gi' them a big send-off. We'll go late on when they're all away in."

Which is why at eleven clock the night before Guy Fawkes, Malcolm and me are quietly climbing out of our bedroom window onto the shelter underneath and then down the drainpipe and away up the street to Bywell Road.

"I canna see where I'm going," I whisper to Mal as we pass through the cut into the swing park.

He hisses back, "Here, look, just follow this." He's brought the bike lamp from under our bed and starts shining it on the ground in front of us. We walk Indian file to the heap we can just about make out at the other side of the park.

If Bells the removal people had seen Malcolm at work that night they would have offered him a job on the spot. He's got it all organised. First trip he takes a kitchen table down from the pile, turns it upside down and starts laying wood and branches on top so we can carry it back between us. Second trip he finds a blanket to tip things in. Third trip I'm starting to flag and I'm yards behind Mal when we get to the park. I see a beam moving way across on my left.

"What you doing over there?" I'm whispering. The beam disappears then seems to come on again in front of me like Malcolm has suddenly turned into The Flash. His voice comes from the second place.

"Howay, hurry up."

"I think there's somebody watching," I warn him as I come up.

"Right, let's make this the last. Here. Move it!"

And I'm hell for leather out of the park with an old deck chair flapping and clacking against my legs.

Back in bed I can't get to sleep for all the excitement of the raid, but my brother zonks out quick enough and he takes some waking an hour or so later.

"Mal, what's that light outside? Malcolm, man!"

He only stirs when I accidentally knee him in the cheek as I climb over to pull the curtain back.

"Ow! What you think you're doing?"

"Look!"

"What?" He struggles up behind me and looks out of the window. "Bloody hell!"

Down in the back garden our biggest bonfire ever is blazing in the night. Revenge is sweet for the Bywell Road gang.

The next morning, Guy Fawkes Day, we're both sitting on the back doorstep staring miserably at the remains when the bin men arrive. Big Hek pops his head round the gate.

"Aye, aye. Got some comics for you two."

Big Hek who works on the bins is an adopted cousin twice removed or whatever, some relation anyway. I thought for a long time naturally enough that he was called Big Hek 'cause he's about the size of a barrage balloon, till I found out his oldest son's called Hek, who gets Little Hek though he's a beefer as well. What Hek stands for I couldn't tell you.

We don't have that much to do with them because, as poor as we are, Mam reckons we're a cut above. But

Big Hek's canny enough and every so often he brings round a pile of Toppers or Beanos or sometimes even DC Comics that folk have put out to their bin.

"Your dad was telling us about your present from Uncle Barney. You'll be excited about the night, eh?"

We just point out the heap of ashes, which Hek looks at with an expert eye, then he hears the story, gives us the comics and gets on with his round.

Come three o'clock, him and his marrers are back with the wagon and a ton of stuff they've hauled off the tip. It's like the scene in the cowboy pictures when everything looks lost and suddenly you hear the bugle and the cavalry turns up. In less than fifteen minutes Big Hek and his mates build us a new bonfire.

"Mind, I expect an invite to your fireworks show," he says, sweating like a galloway pony when it's all done.

Sure enough he arrives, along with Little Hek and Cousin Mo, a few fireworks in one pocket to add to the ones we've got from Uncle Barney and a bottle of whisky in the other that he starts offering around to the grown-ups while we get the bonfire going.

A funny thing about my dad is, although he's never out of the clubs when he's not on shift, he doesn't really drink at home. But with Hek bringing a bottle over he decides to get out the stuff they've got stashed away for people coming at New Year. Pretty soon all the adults are getting tight at the top of the garden and we've got more than enough bottles to fire rockets out of.

It's a brilliant atmosphere. My big sisters are all there with their husbands or boyfriends. Our Jeannie's shuggied in the family's arms till she's dizzy. Everybody's laughing and joking, drinking, and eating taties we've baked in some hot ashes from the bonfire.

We're running back and forward with fireworks from Uncle Barney's box, open on the path. Even the Catherine Wheels work properly for a change.

Malcolm finds an outsize Jumpy Jack and sets it off. It cracks once and leaps up at him. It cracks again.

"It's gone in the box!" shouts Mal.

"What?"

"The Jumpy Jack. It's away into Uncle..."

He doesn't finish. There's a flash from Uncle Barney's box and a rocket comes shooting out and smacks against the coalhouse door. Another flash and a bang and suddenly all hell's let loose. The box is alive with fireworks going off in all directions. Rockets, bangers, flares, sparks, star bombs... everything's flying out of there and we're all scattering, trying to escape.

For two minutes it's complete mayhem. Fireworks screech, swoop and crash around us, over us, under us... it's like a cross between the Valentine's Day Massacre and the Battle of Britain.

Then everything stops and all we can hear is the crackle of the bonfire. Not a soul speaks for what seems like ages. We're looking at each other, not quite believing what just happened. Then Big Hek says, "Anybody hurt?"

We all look around, checking and shaking our heads. Till my sister Rose shouts out, "A Jumpy Jack went right up my skirt."

And everybody collapses, giggling and hysterical. Suddenly it's the funniest thing that's ever happened in our lives and we can't wait to tell each other all about it.

When things quieten down a bit I start rooting through the remains of Uncle Barney's box. I pull out what's left of the big Mine of Serpents, which is all black and charred now.

"Ah, I was saving that till last."

I hold it up to the others. "Did anybody see this one go off? What was it like?"

They all turn round and look at me. Then for some reason everybody bursts out laughing again. They aren't laughing at me, though. It's friendly, natural - we all belong in it, like a family photo. That's what the fireworks people should put on their box lids. They'd sell a million.

ELDERS AND BETTERS

Tenderfoot

Alan Chisholm got me to join the cubs. He'd already been in about two years as his dad was a policeman and he told Alan he wouldn't have him raking the streets. So when we started to be friends at school it wasn't long before he got me to go along with him.

Alan was tall like his dad and I reckon we must have looked funny walking along together 'cause one time we were passing two factory lasses and one nudges the other giggling and blurts out, "Talk about the long and the short of it." The good thing was, though, Alan had already grown out of his first cub uniform so he passed it on to me.

Our Malcolm wasn't impressed. "What's all these dints in the jersey?" he says, picking at them while I'm at Mam's wardrobe mirror trying to get my woggle straight.

"It's just where Alan's badges was. He had to take them off to sew onto his new one."

"It's like you've been whadyacallit, court martialled," says Mal. "Lost your stripes. Is this one of Mam's scarfs?"

"You know what it is, it's a neckerchief. Leave us alone, will ya?"

"Keep your hair on, sissy," Mal snorts.

I wasn't fussed about him. I liked the cubs. Tuesdays we did the laws of the wolf cub pack and learned knots and stuff. Friday was best, though. That was games night and we got to do wrestling and British Bulldog. Bagheera used to take games night. His real name was Simon and he was maybe just a bit older than our Eddie but not hard-looking. More Buddy Hollyish.

Bagheera looked after me from the start at the cubs, making sure I was OK and not left out of things with being the tenderfoot. That's what they call the new boy in the cubs, he told me.

It was Bagheera's idea for me to do a solo at the carol service in St Mark's. The cubs used the hall next door so for Christmas we had to do a church parade and join in the singing. Turns out Bagheera plays the organ for the church so a few weeks before the service he starts us practising these carols on cub night while he picks out the tunes on an old piano next to the stage. We're just finishing one night when he sends Alan off with the others and keeps me behind.

"You know, you have a really sweet voice," he says. "Lovely boy treble."

"I like singing," I tell him. It was true. I was always singing along to the records on our radiogram, and to the songs Uncle Mac played on Saturday morning and Family Favourites on Sunday. And I liked the carols that Bagheera taught us.

"Which one do you like best?" he asks.

"Dunno. Once in Royal David's City?"

"Perfect choice. Come on, sing it with me."

And he pulls me in close to the piano so I can read off the sheet while he plays the music. He joins in at first, then he leaves me to go solo while he plays, smiling to himself and kind of breathing the words in as I sing.

Which is how I end up getting picked to do two verses of Once in Royal David's City all on my own at the carol service. Name in the programme and everything. The church is absolutely packed but there's nobody I know there except Alan and the other cubs. I haven't mentioned it at home 'cause apart from buying The War Cry in the

Comrades every Saturday night my dad can't stick church people and anyway Malcolm would have just taken the piss and more than likely come along specially to make farting noises in the middle of it.

As it is, it's dead quiet when I start singing. Even the organ doesn't play until the rest of the people join in so there's just my voice trying to fill the church on the first verse. I can hear it going up into the roof like it's some kind of starved bird, then it sort of hangs while everybody takes a breath and comes in on *Mary was that mother mild*, making my heart jump.

Afterwards Bagheera comes down from the organ and gives me a squeeze and Akela, who's never spoken to me on my own before, says I've made him proud of the uniform and asks if I'm going to get a new one for Christmas.

It's strange to be walking home so quiet after all the bustle and chatter at the end of the service. It's cold and there's nobody about in our street. The coal wagon must have come earlier in the day. You can tell by the stray pieces of coal that have been left in the gutter, twinkling with the frost forming on them.

Our front room curtains are closed and the light is on behind. The only decorations I can see from outside are two crepe paper bells hanging in the space between the curtain and the window. I suppose it's those and the frost and the thought of the carol service that make me feel like singing again. I stand a foot away from our door and start softly, eyes down to the step.

Once in Royal David's city
Stood a lowly cattle shed
Where a mother laid her baby
In a manger for his bed.

By the time I get to the bit where the people joined in at the church I'm singing with my head up and it's as if I'm in the middle of a crowd of carol singers who I'm hearing behind and around me, filling out the sound, so that when the song ends I can feel the wave of it rolling into the dark for ages. Then it goes silent again and it's just me standing to attention, watching the front door. Which stays shut.

After a couple of minutes the cold gets to my hands and I shove them into the pockets of my khaki shorts, still watching the door. My fingertips are numb but I can feel something in my right pocket and I pick it out to see what it is. It's half a crown, new enough to shine slightly in the light from the moon. I cradle the coin in my palm and stare at it for a while, wondering where it's come from. I take a step back and look across at the front window. I look behind me. I look up at the night sky. Then I slip the money into my pocket and walk around the side of the house to let myself in at the back door.

Inside, my mam's on her own, darning one of my dad's thick pit socks, listening to Wilfred Pickles on the wireless. She looks up briefly as I come in, but doesn't say anything, just goes back to her work. I'm on my way to the bedroom to hide my half crown when I remember the laws of the wolf cub pack and come downstairs again.

"See this half crown, Mam? I found it in my pocket. It was just kind of ...there. Weird."

Mam stops to bite off a thread as she considers the coin in my hand. When she speaks, her eyes are still on it. "Mystery solved. You didn't bring me enough change back when you went for the groceries on Saturday. I meant to ask you about that, but I forgot. Must have left it in your pocket by accident." She goes back to her darning as she says, "Pop it in my purse, there's a good lad."

I can't work out why I'd be wearing my khakis on Saturday but I can't think where else the money could have come from so I'm not about to argue with her.

Instead I take the chance to ask for something I want. As I'm going back up to bed I say, "Would I maybe be able to get a new cub uniform for Christmas this year?"

Mam doesn't look up as she says, "That wouldn't be fair on your brother, would it?"

"But Malcolm's not in the cubs."

"Exactly."

I try to puzzle this one out as I'm going up to bed. On the landing I turn and give Mam the wolf cub salute. Except the downstairs door's shut so she can't see it.

Next cub night Bagheera comes over to me and asks if I've spent my money yet. I haven't a clue what he's on about till he says, "Did you not find anything in your pocket after the carol service?" Then I remember the half crown and tell him I gave it to my mam.

"That was for you, silly," he tuts, chucking me under the chin to get me to look up at him. "Just a little thank you for singing so beautifully. Next time keep it for yourself, eh?"

I decide not to tell Mam she's made a mistake.

It's the last games night before we break up for Christmas so Bagheera tells us we can play Sentries. How it works is our team has to sit out in the porch while the other team makes obstacles from chairs and tables piled together and ropes strung across the hall. Then they have to put all the lights out and creep behind the barriers, waiting for us.

Our job is to crawl from the porch door right through the hall and onto the stage without getting tagged by any of the sentries. Bagheera's the leader of our team. He gets everybody to lie on the floor then turns the porch light off before he starts sending people in one by one. Every time a boy goes through he closes the door again and we lie in the dark listening for sounds in the hall, trying to work out where the guards might be.

Alan's nearly the last sent in so there's just me and Bagheera left lying on the porch floor, waiting our turn. He's behind with his hand on my leg ready to give me the signal to go. Instead he whispers, "You scared?"

"A bit, yeah," I whisper back, but I'm just funning. It's only a game.

"No need to be," he carries on. "Not with me here. We don't have to go in if you don't want, you know. We can just stay here if you like."

As he talks he brings his hand up the back of my leg right to the nick of my bum. A shiver goes through me and without meaning to I jerk my leg, scraping my shoe down the side of his face and hitting against his shoulder. I jump up and clatter through the doorway straight into a pile of chairs.

"Gotcha," calls Tony Dunn, tagging me from inside the pile.

At the end of the night Bagheera keeps me back again. He has a nasty-looking scrape under one leg of his glasses so I know I'm going to get wrong.

"I'm sorry, Bagheera," I start. "I didn't mean to kick..."

"No, that's all right, just an accident. I think we got ourselves a bit mixed up there in the dark. Look," he says, taking a coin from his pocket, "I know you were very good and gave your mam that money I meant for you, but I do want you to have something for yourself. Here, put this towards your Christmas box."

He reaches out for my wrist with one hand and presses the coin into my fingers with the other. His palm feels clammy and I have that shiver again. I pull away from him and the coin falls between us onto the floor.

"No thanks, Bagheera. I'm... I've got plenty for Christmas. You can ... put it in the collection plate."

And I run away from him through the door and up the path by the side of the church to catch up with Alan.

For Christmas I get a scout knife with three blades and a thing for taking stones out of horses' hooves. No new uniform though.

One day in the holidays a letter drops through our front door addressed to me. It's on ordinary writing paper except there's a printed stamp on the top like you can make with one of them John Bull outfits. The stamp has Ashington Hirst Scouts & Wolf Cubs on it.

The letter is to tell me I can't come back to the cubs next term. It says, 'Because of pressure on places it has been decided that priority must be given to regular attendees of St Mark's Sunday School.' At the bottom it's signed S. P. Smythe (BAGHEERA).

Funny enough Alan Chisholm didn't get a letter even though he never went to the Sunday School either. Then again he had been to the cubs much longer than me and had loads of proficiency badges and everything so that's why he'd be OK.

I missed the cubs but the way it turned out I was glad Mam hadn't gone and spent money on a new uniform. Anyway, there was camping weekends and all sorts Alan had to pay for later so it was just as well I was out of it by then. It would have only caused bother at home.

Should Auld Acquaintance

It was great having Eddie back. Of course that meant me having to top and toe with little Jeannie over the Christmas as us lads couldn't fit three in a bed any more, but I didn't mind – it was just nice to see him around the house again.

One of the things I liked about Eddie was that he was the only one in the family who wasn't scared of Dad. Hadn't been since before he left school and there was the ruction about the outside toilet door. I was too young to remember this, but our Rose sometimes talks about it and Malcolm claims he was there.

Seems Eddie is messing about with a line and sinker in the back garden one Saturday, just casting the line out to see how far he can make it reach, when he's caught short and goes to the netty in the yard. While he's sitting there staring at the lavvy door it suddenly occurs to him to try a daft experiment. This is typical Eddie. Hard as he is, he's always had this curiosity about him, always exploring, taking clocks apart to see what makes them tick, that sort of thing.

What he's worked out as he sits contemplating on the bog is that if he loops his line around the bolt on the inside of the door then pushes the sinker through the vent in the side wall he could go round and lock the toilet door from the outside by pulling on the line.

So just to satisfy himself this idea will work that's

exactly what he does. The trouble being, of course, that once he's done it there's no way of undoing it so he snaps the line at the vent and saunters off to amuse himself somewhere else.

We hardly ever went to that outside lavvy as we had an inside one upstairs. Plus Mam only ever put newspaper in the outside one, not proper toilet roll, so we'd only go there in emergencies. Except for my dad.

On this Saturday night, same as every Saturday night when he's not on shift, he staggers home from the club about eleven through the back gate and reaches out in the dark for the sneck of the lavvy door, expecting to relieve himself before he goes into the house. But this time the door doesn't budge. And it stays shut no matter how hard he hammers at it.

Rose is about ready for her bed when she hears these banging noises outside and opens the back door to investigate, just in time to happen on Dad pissing in the bin corner.

Naturally he's mortified at one of his own girls seeing him like this and mad as hell about the locked door so by the time he comes inside he's raging. Eddie's still up, trying to tune in Luxembourg on the wireless, and Dad goes straight for him.

Why he's figured Ed's to blame I don't know – maybe he's just the obvious one in the room to hit out at, which he does, first with a mighty smack around the ear then, while Eddie's still reeling, Dad's off with his belt and sets himself to launch a right good thrashing.

Only this time my big brother stands up to him. As the belt strikes down Ed lifts his arm, lets the strap snake round it and grabs with his hand. For a few seconds, as Rose says when she tells it, it's tug o' war in our living room, with Dad and Eddie either side, hackles up, bracing themselves. Then Eddie gives a sudden pull and comes away with the belt.

Dad's left swaying and panting in the middle of the room and his eldest son's stood looking at him, his fist round the strap. It's like fifteen years has turned on its head when he spits out, "Look at you. You're nowt, you. You're a flamin' disgrace."

He throws the belt aside, sends it clattering into the hearth, then before anybody can say another word Eddie's grabbed his jacket off the banister and he's away out through the front door.

When and how he came back I don't know, but of course he did and things seemed to carry on much as normal. But not really. 'Cause everybody says Eddie changed from that day on. Even though he was with us another two years before he joined the navy it felt like he was just staying in the house, not living there. He always looked as if he was ready to leave. Dad never touched him or raised his voice to him again and Eddie pretty much went his own way. He started buying stuff for himself from catalogues and off adverts on the back of war comics, especially after he got the job on the furniture van. Some chest expanders once, a tinny transistor radio, an air gun.

One Sunday morning he's sitting on the bed with his vest on, holding the air gun, and I'm propped up beside him in my pyjamas, watching. Eddie's taped a row of matches onto the board at the foot of the bed and now he's aiming his gun at them, trying to light them with a direct hit on the match heads. Every so often I have to duck out of the way as a slug comes pinging back off the board.

I feel as if I'm in a cowboy picture and when the bedroom door flings open it could be Wyatt Earp striding into the saloon to break up a fight. Only here the marshal is Dad. He stops in the doorway and stands looking at us, saying nowt for ages, but I can see his knuckles going white where he's gripping the edge of the door. Eddie says nowt neither, just picks another slug off the pile on the bedspread and reloads his gun. Finally Dad points a finger at me.

"You, clothes on right now. Your mam wants you downstairs."

With that he retreats. I'm climbing out of bed when Eddie touches my arm.

"Hang on, youngun," he says. "Watch me get this first."

He aims the gun steadily and fires at the bedpost. A match flares, burning varnish on the board. You can still see the scorch mark years later, a reminder of what my big brother could do.

So now Eddie's back home on leave and that makes Christmas even more special. For a start he buys me and Mal an electric train set, which is easily the best present we've ever had. Then him and my older sisters decide we're going to have a proper party in the house to bring the New Year in, with their friends coming round as well as just family and the neighbours. There'll be music and dancing and party food, not just booze and broth. It'll start when the pubs shut and finish when they open again, says Eddie.

A couple of days before the party he decides we need some new records and he takes me along with him to Oliver's. That's a furniture shop but it has a record department upstairs with a row of booths that are like sentry boxes with little holes in the walls where you can stand and listen to the music before you buy it. He picks It's Only Make Believe, Hoots Mon! and Tom Dooley and lets me get The Chipmunks Song if I promise to mime it for a party piece.

The night of New Year's Eve me and Malcolm are like kennelled dogs waiting for everybody to come back from the pubs and clubs so the do can start. We keep sniffing around in the kitchen where there's pastries under a cloth and a big bowl of trifle. The records are piled up on top of the radiogram but Mam won't let us play any in case they get scratched before Eddie's back to take charge. She does let us have some home-made ginger wine until Mal pretends to get drunk and spills some on the couch, then she takes our glasses away.

At last Rose comes in with Vince and two of her friends from the factory.

"Have you seen owt of your dad?" Mam asks.

"Yeah, he left the White House same time as us. He was going to the Comrades and he said he might look in at the British Legion on the way home."

When Sally and a whole bunch arrive Mam goes next door to seek Auntie Florrie and Uncle George while Rose and Sally set the food out. I take the chance to put Elvis on. Douglas and Vince move the couch to the back wall and Rose's mates face each other to dance that closed-in rock 'n' roll that lasses do when there's no fellers up to fling them about.

"Was Eddie not with you?" Rose asks our Sally.

"He's hooked up with Ivan Rutter – he's on leave an' all. Been on shorts all night so they'll be in a state the morn."

"They'll be back here for midnight though, won't they?"

"Eddie promised they would. Reckons he's got a go-as-you-please organised for later, with prizes and everything." Sally turns to me. "Hey pet, what's this I hear about you doing the Chipmunks?"

While we're waiting for Eddie and my dad the party warms up. Sally lifts the rug so they can dance easier and me and Mal take turns being DJ. Everybody keeps an eye on the clock so we don't forget to put the wireless on for Big Ben.

At quarter to twelve Dad suddenly appears from the kitchen. Having the music so loud, we've not heard him come in through the back door. He looks out of place with all the dancing and the banter going on, and he stands on the edge of it, not taking his jacket off or speaking even when Mam asks, "Have you seen our Eddie?" He just shakes his head, walks back into the kitchen where the drinks are and stays there.

Which makes it a bit awkward when midnight strikes 'cause that's when Dad usually takes over, making sure everybody's glass is full and leading the toast and the singing. There's a bit of confusion before our Sally's Douglas gets us all sorted more or less into a ring. I'm crossing my arms ready to grab Mam's hand when she breaks the circle and calls into the kitchen.

"Howay, Dad. You're missing Auld Lang Syne."

And he does come, placing himself between Mam and me and wrapping his big hand around mine while we all sing half the first verse and tum-ti-tum the rest before crushing each other into the middle of the living room as soon as the chorus starts.

Then it's all giggling and kissing and shaking hands around the room. After that there's a bit of a lull, with people searching for where they set their drinks down while me and Mal's shuffling through the records to find The Chipmunks Song so I can do my party piece. There's a noise at the front door, somebody fumbling with a key in the lock.

"First foot!" shouts Rose. "Is there coal on the step?"

"It'll be our Eddie," says Mam, pleased.

"*He's* not a stranger," comes Rose.

"No, but at least he's dark so that's half good luck anyway."

The living room door swings open and there's Eddie, with Ivan Rutter close behind. Auntie Florrie's sitting with her back to the door and as she turns she raises her sherry glass calling out, "Happy New Year!"

She's the only one. The rest of us are staring at the massive red and blue bruise that's closing Eddie's left eye and the blood on his white collar. He stares back at us, sullen.

Mam breaks the silence, her hand to her mouth, choking up. "What happened?"

"Ask him!" sneers Eddie, pointing at Dad. The knuckles on his hand are white and skinned. "Ask him, he got a good enough view of it. Before he pissed off, like."

He wipes some bloody spit off his mouth, turns and heads up the stairs. Dad walks off the other way, into the kitchen. Mam seems caught in the middle for a second then follows Dad, closing the door behind her.

"What's all this about?" Douglas asks Ivan, who's still standing half in the passage. Ivan's shirt's ripped below his tie as if somebody's grabbed at it.

"We were in the Legion," he says. "Some big army bastard picks a fight with Ed 'cause he reckons he's got a cocky look on him. I was gonna dive in but this bloke's marrers held us back. Eddie got a right twattin'."

"What's his dad got to do with it?"

"He came in just as it all kicked off. He took one look and he was off out the door. Buggered off and left them to it."

"He'll have not realised it was Eddie," says our Rose.

Ivan glances up the stairs. "Try telling Eddie that. He says he looked him straight in the eyes. Looked him straight in the eyes and walked out."

And that's just what my big brother did that New Year's morning. Walked out, same as he had the night Dad tried to belt him. Except this time he didn't come back the next day. Nor the day after. He was at Ivan's place for the rest of his leave, then he went back to the navy and didn't bother coming home for a long time. Not for years, to tell you the truth.

If this had been a film, my dad would have stepped in to save Eddie from the bashing he got. Then everything that had happened in the past between them would have been forgiven. Should auld acquaintance be forgot and never brought to mind. But this wasn't a film. Or a song.

Light Fingers

"Right. Which one of you's been in my purse?"

Malcolm and me are side by side on the couch where Mam's ordered us to sit while she stands in front of the mantelpiece with her arms folded looking from one to the other, waiting for an answer.

"Not me," says Malcolm.

Which can't be true 'cause I know it isn't me. Not today, anyway. Not since I pinched half a crown for my bus fare to Plessey Woods the time I was going to run away. And that was ages ago.

Malcolm turns his head. "You're not saying much."

"Don't start getting me blamed," I whinge, kicking at his foot with mine. "You know I didn't do it."

"How does he know?" demands Mam. She's like Perry Mason jumping on your words so I shut up again.

"Well?"

I say nothing and we're all three held in prickly silence for a minute, her looking down at us, him and me looking away. Then Malcolm says, "How much was it?"

"You know very well how much it was," comes Mam. "There's a ten shillin' note missing. How am I supposed to manage without?"

That's a lot. I glance sideways at Malcolm. What's he been wanting that costs ten bob?

"Are you listening? I said - how am I supposed to manage?"

"Dunno." I'm snivelling and the word doesn't come out properly. Malcolm shrugs and stares down at his sandshoes.

Mam breathes in and tightens her arms across her chest. "That's all you've got to say, is it? We'll just have to wait till your dad comes in, then. See what *he* can get out of the pair of you."

Malcolm looks up sharp. "Don't tell me dad."

"What else am I supposed to do?" She turns away, irritated, and catches sight of herself in the mirror over the fireplace. She grabs the hairbrush that's lying on the mantelpiece. I press against the back of the couch, frightened she'll bray us with it, but instead she starts brushing hard at her hair in front of the mirror. For a while the only sound in the room is this brush going through her hair. Then she puts it down and picks up the blue ornament that our Sally brought her from Blackpool.

"See this jug? I'm going to look in here on Sunday morning and I expect to find a ten shillin' note in it. If I don't you'll have your dad to answer to." And she plonks the present from Blackpool back on the mantelpiece to show that's her final word on the subject. So we skedaddle.

"What you spent it on?" I ask Malcolm in the back yard.

"I've spent nowt. I didn't nick her frigging money. *You* must've."

"I never."

He jumps across and forces my head under his armpit, searching through my pockets with his other hand while I'm wriggling to get away.

"Leave off, will ya? I've got nowt."

He squeezes my neck tighter. "Cross your heart and hope to die?"

"Cross my heart and hope to die," I say, choking.

He keeps me doubled up till I do the sign of the cross over my chest then lets me go, rubbing his arm like he's the one hurt.

"We've got to put it back, anyway," he says. "Or we'll both get the belt."

"Where we going to get ten shilling from before Sunday?"

"What have you got to sell?"

"Nothing." I'm thinking frantically. "Few comics, but that's just swaps."

"We'll have to earn it," says Malcolm. "Like bob-a-job. Let's away and see if Auntie Florrie wants some shopping in."

Auntie Florrie wasn't our real auntie – she was the woman who lived next door - but we'd always called her that, and her husband was Uncle George who worked in the same pit as my dad till he had to finish on account of his lungs. She was forever asking us to do her shopping and usually she'd give us summat out of the change, tuppence or threepence maybe. But if we were going anyway for Mam she'd give us nowt, so we'd try and sneak away without her seeing when we had Mam's groceries to fetch on Saturday mornings.

Uncle George opens the door in his slippers.

"Does Auntie Florrie want any shopping done?" Malcolm asks him.

"Ah, she's not in, son. She's popped down to the Housey at the Arcade. I'll tell her you were asking though, but."

Housey Housey was getting all the rage in Ashington among the women. It just used to be the Trade Union Hall that put it on once a week, but now you could play upstairs at the Arcade every day except Sundays. Auntie Florrie was never away from the place. Uncle George didn't know the half of it, Mam says. Sometimes she'd make on she needed summat at the chemist or was off to see their Peg and she'd end up at the matinée game at the Arcade. I'm glad my mam never bothered with it.

"Shit!" goes Malcolm under his breath, kicking the step after Uncle George has closed the door.

"What about pop bottles?" I suggest.

He turns and clicks his fingers. "Pop bottles," he says. "Howay, there'll be some in the shed."

Generally, though, we'd return bottles to the shop or the pop van as soon as they were finished with, so there's half an hour's rummaging about to do before we come across a couple of grubby ones that's been used for firing rockets out of on bonfire night. I'm not convinced Matteson's will take them back even after we've run them under the tap. Anyway, that's only tuppence, a long way off our target.

On the way to Matteson's we bump into Derek Nesbitt and tell him what we're up to, except we don't mention the missing ten bob or it'll be the talk of the neighbours in no time.

"You should get yoursel's round the back o' the Comrades if you're wanting bottles," comes Nez. "You'll have to wait till it's dark, like."

Bringing Nez in means a three-way split but we're desperate for the cash and he's the one with the know-how so that's why we end up with him that night looking through the fence into the yard at the back of the Comrades Social Club.

There's some metal barrels in the yard and crate upon crate of empties, mostly Newcastle Brown or Amber Ale, but Nez points out a stack of cardboard boxes for lemonade bottles next to the wall by a drainpipe.

"See, they're all waiting to go back to Waters and Robsons. No harm done if we just take them to the shops first."

Fair play to Nez, it's him that volunteers to go over the fence since he's done it before, so Malcolm and me give him a bunk up and he drops quietly down on the other side. First thing he does is roll one of the metal barrels next to the fence beside us, then he sneaks across to the stack of lemonade bottles.

We stand on the other side of the fence stretching up for the boxes while Nez stands on the barrel passing them over. There's a dozen bottles in each box so they're pretty heavy and we have to be careful not to tip them out as we bring them down on our finger ends from the top of the fence.

By the time Nez has made three visits to the stack we're all working smoothly and quickly. He's just easing the fourth lot over the spikes when a door opens in the wall behind him. In the light of the doorway we can see a man carrying two boxes, just like the one Nez in his panic is pushing hard towards us. We reach up but the box tips over and twelve empty bottles come raining down past Mal and me to smash around our feet.

"Hey!" shouts the bloke from the doorway. He puts his load down but by the time he's run across to the fence Nez has scrambled over it, crunching on broken glass, and we scarper up the alley with the rest of our bottles bobbing and rattling as we go.

Next day we cart the bottles across to the shops. We reckon it'll be suspicious if we take them all to Matteson's so we split them up around three different shops, though twelve is still a lot to take in at once.

The last place is called Ogilvie's, a corner shop like Rodway's but dirtier and even more crowded with stuff so the counter's more like a hatch. There's a man with a grey overall at the hatch, Mr Ogilvie I suppose.

"You been saving these up?" he asks when we hand the box of pop bottles over. Mal has his answer ready.

"We've been collecting round the doors. Me mam's electric iron broke and we're trying to get enough money to buy her a new one, for a surprise."

"By, I wish I had canny kids like you. Keen as mustard, an' all. Here," he pokes his head through the hatch and drops his voice low, "I'd like to help you out. You know them coupons you can cut off packets of soap powder and that? You bring me as many as you can lay your hands on and I'll give you cash, half what it says on the coupons. But not a word to anybody, right? It's just my way of helping you get that iron for your mam."

We're delighted at this. With having to give a third of the money from the pop bottles to Nez we've only made two bob plus the tuppence from the ones in the shed, so we badly needed another money-making idea.

We run home. Lucky enough Mam's in the living room having a cup of tea with Auntie Florrie so we can spoach around the kitchen and the pantry without being disturbed. The bad news is we don't come up with much. There's a 3d voucher we cut off a packet of Ajax cleaning powder. We find a dividend coupon for 5d under the lid of an Oxo Cube tin. And that's it until Malcolm opens a drawer and finds a collecting card for Black & Greens tea with all but two of the stamps filled in. You get 5/- back off the full card, so we reckon Mr Ogilvie might give us two bob for the card as it is.

"Hang on," I says to Malcolm as he's taking the card out of the drawer. "We'll get into trouble about this an' all."

"Aggh, she'll just think she's forgotten where she put it," Mal comes back. "Anyway, it's not like nicking real money, is it? Same as the pop bottles."

I'm about to argue when our Rose suddenly comes in through the back way. Malcolm quickly shoves the dividend card up his jersey and shuts the drawer. We'd forgotten she finishes half an hour earlier on a Friday.

"What are you two skulking round here for?"

"We're not skulking," says Mal. "We're just looking for string to finish a kite off." I've always been amazed at my brother's talent for making up honest-sounding lies without missing a beat.

We manage to get away from Rose and across to the shops again to see Mr Ogilvie. He'll only give us one and nine for the tea stamps and fourpence for the coupons so we've now got a grand total of four shilling and threepence and only one more full day to make up the rest.

"Let's put what we've got so far in the jug to show willing," says Mal, which we do on the quiet 'cause Dad's in the house by now and we don't want him asking questions.

That night in bed we're racking our brains for a scheme to raise the five bob and more we still need. Mal even wonders whether we should go begging on the street corner like the old bloke who draws pictures on the pavement next to the market. But that man's got no legs plus he's doing summat for his money and he still never seems to have much in his cap, so what chance have we got?

After all the talking we've made no plans by the time Malcolm turns on his side to try and get some sleep. I'm left staring into the darkness, still working out how we can make up the difference.

"You know it's not fair. We shouldn't have to be doing this," I say out loud. There's no response from Malcolm. I turn to look over at him, lying there quite peaceful.

"Malcolm?" No answer. "I bet you did nick that ten bob."

A back-heel comes hard under the blankets, catching me right in the balls.

Saturday morning I'm up before everybody else. I'm thinking, if I go early and get Mam's groceries in, *one* it might put her in a better mood for what happens tomorrow and *two* it will give us the rest of the day to go round the doors asking if anybody wants their gardens weeded or their coals putting in.

I'm just fetching the shopping bags from the kitchen when I see Auntie Florrie passing the window to get to our back door. She'll be wanting us to pick her stuff up as well. If I make on I'm already gone she might pay us to go back later for hers. I grab the bags and run to hide in the passage.

"Anybody in? It's only me," she says as she slides in soft as a ferret at the back door. I can't hear anybody stirring in the bedrooms. I watch through the crack in the door in case Auntie Florrie's coming through to call at the foot of our stairs. But she stops when she gets to the living room and stands looking about.

She spots a brown envelope on the mantelpiece and just stretches a couple of fingers out as if she's trying to check what's inside without really disturbing it. That'll be our Rose's pay packet left from when she opened it to give mam her board. There'll be nowt in there 'cause Rose went to the hop last night.

I can see Auntie Florrie's face in the mirror over the fireplace. This early in the morning she's not put her makeup on and she looks all pinched and pale. As I'm watching, her head goes up an inch or two as if she's floating off the floor. Then I realise she's up on her tippy-toes, her hand on the mantelpiece. She reaches out with her other hand and pulls the Blackpool jug towards her. That's where our money is.

When she looks round at the door I get a gliff, thinking she must see me through the crack, but she turns away again and in few seconds she empties the cash out of the jug, puts it in her pinny pocket, replaces the jug and leaves the house as quietly as she came in.

I'm still staring into the empty room when I realise I haven't breathed from the time she peeked into Rose's pay packet until now. I'm blushing beetroot red as if it was me that was stealing the money and I've just been caught. But it was my Auntie Florrie. And very likely it was her that lifted my mam's ten shilling note.

I stand for ages, trying to figure out what to do. Somehow I don't want to tell on Auntie Florrie but if I don't say anything to Malcolm he'll think it's me that's emptied the jug. I've got no choice but to sneak up the stairs and tell him what's gone on.

Malcolm's all for squealing to Mam straight away. I'm not so sure.

"I don't know, she might not believe us. Anyway, it'll cause a big row."

"You'd rather we just got the belt, would you, let her get away with it? She's nicked our money an' all, remember."

"I know but, they're friends an' that. An' she's still gonna have to live next door to us."

"Aye, so she can keep on doing it and we'll keep getting the blame. That's champion that is," sneers Malcolm.

We're still arguing about it while we're lugging Mam's groceries from the shops but by the time we're back home I've persuaded Mal to do the last thing in the world we want to do except that anything else would be worse. Which is to go round and see Auntie Florrie ourselves.

I'm ending myself as Mal rattles their knocker. Just like the other day Uncle George opens the door and a big part of me is wishing he's going to say she's not in again. But she is.

"Hello, lads," he says cheerfully. "I told your Auntie Florrie you're keen to do her messages. Got a few bits' 'n' pieces she's wanting. Howay in."

And he shepherds us through the door into their living room.

"Florrie!" he shouts up the stairs. "Here's the laddies from next door for you. Sit yoursel's down, boys."

"We'll just stand, thanks," mutters Malcolm. We wait side by side on their rug with our hands behind us like we're about to get told off, while Uncle George goes back to his newspaper.

When Auntie Florrie comes down the stairs I notice she's put her makeup on. She's carrying her purse in her hand.

"I thought I'd missed the boat when I saw you out of our window with your mam's shopping," she says, smiling. "Ta for coming by."

I nudge Malcolm. He clears his throat.

"Em, it's not about the shopping, Auntie Florrie."

"Oh, right."

"It's about..." Mal falters, for once having to search for his words. I have to step in.

"It's about the blue jug," I say. "The jug from Blackpool. You know ... on our mantelpiece."

Out of the corner of my eye I can see Uncle George look up from his paper, vaguely wondering why I'm talking gibberish. But mainly I'm watching Auntie Florrie and how she goes pale again even under that makeup, and her eyes widen.

"Oh," is all she says before she sits down on the arm of their settee. What I'm saying next is really for Uncle George 'cause she already knows the rest.

"Just ... well, that was our money. And I saw you taking it."

Mal chips in, more confident now. "And we know about the ten bob note. We was getting the blame for it."

Auntie Florrie looks down to our toes. "I know you were. I know you were," she says, really faint. "Your mam was telling us yesterday."

Uncle George is taking proper notice now, looking concerned. "What's all this about? Florrie?"

Auntie Florrie is hiding her head from all three of us. She doesn't answer Uncle George at first. She's fumbling under the sleeve of her cardigan for a hankie and we watch a tear splashing onto her wrist before she gets it out.

"Florrie?" Uncle George says again.

"Oh, George, I've been stealing from next door," says Auntie Florrie all in a rush at last. "I stole some money from Bella. And from these little kiddies..."

At which she breaks down into full tears. Uncle George looks lost for a moment then he does something I never expected, maybe because I was thinking just then what my dad would do. He goes over and wraps Auntie Florrie up in his arms as if she's a little girl who's hurt herself and she's sobbing against his chest. I've got tears filling as well, like I have whenever Malcolm is getting smacked or belted and I'm just standing by.

Next thing Auntie Florrie's owning up to Uncle George about the Housey Housey. She's telling him she's been dipping into the housekeeping and just lately she's been running three cards to try and win back the money she's lost, and how that's made things worse.

"I didn't want to have to tell you," she says. "I thought if I could just win one Full House I'd be able to put all the money back and nobody'd be any the wiser. I was going to give it all up, George, honest. As soon as I got square with the money, I was going to pack it all in."

Uncle George strokes her head and shushes her until she's quiet again. He turns to us and says, "You did right, lads. You did a brave thing coming round. Now, would you do us one little favour? Would you mind just popping home and letting your mam know your Auntie Florrie would like a word? No need to say anything else at all. Will you do that for us?"

Malcolm and me leave quietly. We say nothing to each other till we've climbed the fence between the two back gardens. Then Mal turns to me. "Bloody hell," is all he says.

Mam's steeping clothes when we get back and she doesn't look too pleased about having to pop next door or about anything else come to think. As she's going out she gives us a firm look and says, "I've got another bone to pick with you two. Our Rose tells me you were in that kitchen drawer last night. When I come back I want to know what you've done with that dividend card. And I don't want to hear any more of your lies."

"I told you we'd be in bother over them stamps," I hiss at Malcolm when she's gone. Mal sticks his mouth under the kitchen tap, slurps a drink and wipes his mouth with a big sweep of his hand like Popeye after he's had his spinach. He turns to me with a grin.

"We'll not be in any bother," he says. "Not this time."

And he was right.

Steady

The trouble for Vince began around the time Rose was old enough to have her own Provi cheque. I don't just mean that's how she met Peter, though that was an important part of it, more that she started to think in grown-up ways, especially about how things might work out in the future, which of course meant her and Vince. Or not.

Mam wasn't that struck on Vince but the rest of us liked him, even Dad. He said you knew where you stood with him. Maybe they got on so well 'cause Vince went down the pit straight from school, same as him.

One of the things I liked about Vince was he took notice of you but he knew when to leave you alone. Say for example I'd be sitting on the step when he arrived, hacking mud off my football boots. Nine times out of ten he'd pick me up, turn me upside down and maybe swing me round the yard for a laugh. But if another time he came in and I was head down in a story book or listening to Dan Dare on the wireless he might just give a little grin or tousle my hair a bit, not to disturb. Even though he wasn't one for reading himself.

He'd make funny faces on the sly at me while Rose was going on at him, which she did a lot. Apart from moaning about his lads' nights out, her main complaint was over the time he spent with his pigs.

"You think more of your precious pigs than you do of me," she'd always say.

Not that they were really Vince's pigs, but he'd been looking after them for Mr Ellis since he was a kid at school. Ellis's place was more like a big allotment than a farm - just the pig sty, a few chickens plus a horse and cart that Vince let me ride with him sometimes when he went to pick up pig swill from school canteens and the like.

"Hi-yo Silver, away," we'd yell to the knackered old grey to make her go.

Our Rose went spare the day me and him went round to see if we could spot her coming out from the factory. She'd got some overtime in on Saturday morning and he'd taken me to feed the horse at Ellis's place.

"It's nearly twelve," he says. "Howay, let's give Silver a run out by Culpitts."

Silver's friskier than usual. She gets a fair gallop on down Stakeford Bank and Vince has to rein her in to keep the cart steady. We're rattling along over the railway crossing at North Seaton when we spy three factory lasses in the distance, linking arms the way they do. Vince gees up Silver some more and sure enough when we get near we see it's Rose flanked by two of her workmates. Vince draws the cart alongside them and touches his flat cap.

He goes, "How-de-do. Would you young ladies care for a lift?"

The ginger one nearest us bursts out laughing and the fat lass on the other side squeezes on Rose's arm. My sister doesn't look right pleased to see us.

"We're not getting up on that rig," she sneers at Vince. "Get away with it."

Back home she's even worse on poor Vince. "Are you trying to show me up?"

"Just came to say hello."

"D'you know what Jean Evans said when you went up the road? Are you going to ride to your wedding on that? They were skittin' me."

"What wedding?"

"Exactly what I was thinking. Plus, do you have to wear that great long coat and the cap?"

"It's just my stuff for pigging out," says Vince, spreading his arms out and looking down at himself.

"It smells like it an' all," cries Rose. "Coming round here straight out of a pig sty. You're a right catch dressed like that, aren't ya? I don't know what I'm going to do wi' you."

He looks at me sideways and pulls a face. It's all I can do not to start giggling while Rose has gone the other way, dabbing a hankie at her eyes.

"Tell you one thing for nothin'. If you think you're going steady wi' me you're gonna have to buck your ideas up. And smarten up. Or else."

She glares out the window like she's weighing up chucking Vince out on the street there and then. He mimics her face and mouths *or else* at me. I'm biting my finger so hard it hurts.

It's the idea of smartening him up that decides Rose on getting out her first-ever Provident cheque so she can buy Vince a posh new coat for a birthday surprise. She trails me along with her to Doggarts 'cause Mam says I'm desperate for shoes.

In the men's department we're flicking along the coat racks when this lad about Vince's age steps up to help.

"Anything in particular you're after?" Pretty stupid question seeing as we're rummaging through men's coats. But Rose doesn't seem to mind him.

"Oh, a new coat," she says. "Gent's."

"For this young man?" looking down at me. "Children's clothes are down..."

"Ah, no. It's for my... for a friend's birthday. It's a surprise."

"Lucky feller, that's what I say," he puts in, grinning at Rose. I'm reckoning now he's probably a year or so older than Vince. Both tall, bigger than Rose anyway, but they're like chalk and cheese otherwise. I suppose his sharp suit comes with the job, same with the shirt and tie, but it's not just the clothes. There's his slick hair parting and even his hands running over that row of coats. Smooth, not with any of them little blue marks that Vince and my dad both have on their knuckles, very faint like the colour's under the skin.

"These Burberrys are very stylish," he's saying. "Very *in* just now. What size might we be looking for?"

I'm thinking of Vince taking his voice off, *what size might we be looking for?* and I have to put my hand up to my face, making on my nose is itchy.

"About your size," Rose says. "Maybe a wee bit broader. Would you mind trying that one on for me?"

Peter (he's told us his name by this time) tries a few different coats on for Rose, sometimes turning round for her to see all angles, sometimes checking himself in the big mirror, and they get chatting as she's making her mind up.

"Haven't I seen you at the Arcade dance?" he asks her.

"Ee, I thought I knew you from somewhere. I don't go so much now. How about you?"

"Sometimes, but it's usually the Mayfair for me these days. More modern altogether."

"Oh, we never go to Newcastle," she says. "That's like abroad to us. I've heard it's good at the Mayfair, though."

"It shows the Arcade up for what it is, that's for sure. You should come along some time. You'd enjoy it."

I'm bored stupid by the time Rose finally gets around to choosing a navy blue Burberry and Peter's folding it up all neatly for her to take away.

"Oh, you do take Provident cheques here, don't you?" she says, turning a bit red while she's asking. Rosy Rose we call her when she blushes like that.

"Certainly, madam. Miss. Have you got your book on you? It'll just take a minute to sort out."

"He was nice, eh, that Peter?" she says as we're walking home, her with the Doggarts bag, me carrying a shoe box.

"All right, I suppose. Is Vince coming over later?"

"Yeah, I'll have to hide this somewhere. He was smart though, wasn't he? You could tell straight away he's not just a shop assistant. Trainee manager, did you hear him say? Wonder how much it pays, a job like that."

Don't know what she's asking me for.

To be honest, Vince doesn't cover himself in glory on his birthday. Even before Rose gives him his present, he lets her know they won't be able to go out Saturday night. His marrers have organised a pub crawl round Morpeth. They're getting a lift in somebody's van.

Rose whinges. "So what am I supposed to do?"

"I don't know. I can't take you, can I? It's a lads' night out."

"Well, you don't have to go."

"'Course I do. The whole thing's supposed to be for my birthday. No show without Punch."

"Sounds just like you know who," snipes Mam in the background, which doesn't exactly help matters.

In fact everybody's so on edge that when Vince finally gets round to opening up Rose's parcel it's like he's working on an unexploded bomb in the middle of the living room, with the ticking from our mantelpiece clock adding the sound effect while we all watch him in silence.

"Well, aren't you going to try it on?" Rose prompts him once he's lifted the coat out of its wrapping and he's inspecting it at arm's length. He does, but to be fair it doesn't look as good on him as it did on Peter in the shop. It's not so much the coat as the way he's wearing it. Rose can see it as well, even though she acts enthusiastic when she says, "What do you think?"

"It makes us look like an undertaker."

Light the blue touchpaper and stand well back. By the time Rose has dragged the coat off his shoulders and tore into him about how she's hocked herself up to make him look like a half-decent human being, only for him to throw it back in her face, Vince is turning to me for the escape plan. But it's Rose who hits the ejector button.

"So if that's how you feel you can go and have your birthday tea with your filthy, smelly pigs. And you can go and drink yoursel' silly with your mates on Saturday night 'cause I've got better things to be doing anyroad. I don't need you, Vince Logan, there's plenty I could be going out with, so you might as well buzz off."

And with one sorry look at me that's what Vince does. Rose runs up to her bedroom leaving the new Burberry in the middle of the living room floor.

When Rose makes her mind up to take it back to Doggarts, Mam warns her it'll be a right clart trying to get a refund, especially with it being bought on the Provi, but she comes home from the shop without the coat and with a wide smile on her face.

"Peter sorted it out for us, no problem," she says, "And guess what. He's asked me to go to the Mayfair with him on Saturday night."

"You're never going all the way to Newcastle just for a dance," says Mam.

"Why not, when I've got somebody to take me? I've got nowt else to do."

"Has he got a car?" says I.

"Well, no, but he must be paying my bus fare 'cause he said to let the conductor know he'd be getting on at the White Elephant. He lives in Newbiggin Road. They're private houses, aren't they, Mam?"

Saturday morning I go across with some crusts I've been saving for Silver. Vince is there, flinging grain across the yard for the chickens. Soon as I'm up to him he asks, "How's Rose? Is she getting some more overtime in?"

"Not today, no. She's at the hairdressers. She's away out dancing the night."

"What, with your Sally?"

"No, with a lad called Peter."

"Oh." Vince doesn't say anything more for a bit and I watch him spreading the feed, then, "Peter, eh? What's he like?"

"He wears a stripy suit."

"Convict, is he?" says Vince, winking and lobbing a fistful of grain at me.

"No, stupid. I mean like a tailor's dummy."

"Has he been up at the house?"

"No, I seen him at Doggarts."

"In the window?"

"What? Oh," catching on, "No, inside the shop. He works there. He's a trainee manager."

"Ooh, *trainee manager*," says Vince, putting that voice on. He brushes his hands together, dusting the grain away. "Maybe I'll have to take a walk up to Doggarts."

"You gonna fight him, Vince?" I'm little Joey and Vince is Shane.

He looks down at me and ruffles my hair, with a lopsided grin on him.

"I meant I ought to buy myself a suit," he says.

The thing I remember about Rose just before she goes for the bus that Saturday night, as she's lacquering her hair in front of the living room mirror and I'm ducking away from the spray, is how much lipstick and eye stuff she's put on compared to when she goes out with Vince – it's like she's walking out on stage.

Maybe that wouldn't have stuck so much in my memory if it wasn't that the next time I see my sister her lipstick's all skew-whiff and mascara's running down her cheeks from weeping.

It must be after midnight when Mal and me both get woken up by the commotion below. Naturally we charge downstairs to see what's going off and burst in to find Mam somewhere between quizzing and consoling our Rose on the settee while Dad, half-cut, is pacing the room ready to get his mad up.

"Has that lad been trying summat on he shouldn't?" he's saying. "Is that what you're upset about?"

"No, Dad, it's got nowt to do with Peter. It's… it's Vince. I think he's gone in the river," and she starts wailing again.

Mal and me look at each other. Has Vince chucked himself in 'cause of Rose? Then she goes on.

"We were coming back from Newcastle on the last bus and we got stopped at Stakeford Bank. There was a police car with its lights on blocking the bridge. We were stuck there for ages, so the conductor went to see what was what. It was… It was a van crashed through into the river."

"Vince was talking about going with his mates in a van," Mam says, putting her hand to her mouth.

"Whisht, there's lots of vans on the road," says Dad. "'S not tied to be the one Vince is in."

"But the cops told our conductor there was four young lads," sobs Rose. "And they'd been out drinking in Morpeth."

"Jesus," says Mam. "Are they all right?"

94

Rose starts wailing again. "Ah, Mam," she cries, "Two o' them's drowned. Two... Two's gone to hospital."

"Did you get any names?" shouts out Dad. Mam stares hard at him and he sort of wilts, putting his hand up to say sorry. Dad hardly ever says sorry. I nudge Malcolm to see if he's noticed, only that turns out to be a mistake 'cause the movement catches Mam's eye and she looks up at us for the first time, still hard-faced like she was with Dad.

"You two, off to bed now."

Malcolm starts to argue. "Why do we have to...?"

Then Dad butts in. "Now!" he yells, and we beetle up the stairs.

For the next twenty minutes we crouch on the cold landing listening in to the talk downstairs. Rose is telling them the police weren't giving any names and they moved the bus on after a while. Peter was trying to see the van out of the bus window as they passed the bridge, but Rose hid her eyes. He'd got off at the White Elephant since she didn't want him to bring her home. She hadn't even told Peter who she thought was in the van and she'd kept the tears in until she got off the bus at her stop.

After a while there's some moving about which I reckon is Mam putting the kettle on, then Malcolm who has his ear to the floor says, "Dad's going to the hospital."

"What?"

"He just told her he'll go and find out what he can. She's to get off to bed."

Five minutes later the living room door opens and we scatter into our bedroom as somebody comes up the stairs.

On the way to her room Rose comes into ours to say goodnight. Once we know who it is we stop pretending to be asleep and sit up. Mal pokes his head through the curtains to watch for Dad going out to the hospital while

I sit with Rose as she sips her cocoa on the edge of our bed. She's fixed her makeup and calmed down a bit, but she's still pale and mournful.

"Do you think Vince was in that van?" I ask her.

"I don't know, love. Let's hope not, eh? We'll keep our fingers crossed."

And I do right there, but under the blanket so Malcolm can't see.

"I like Vince, you know, Rose," I say.

"I know you do, sweetheart."

Suddenly Malcolm's hissing at us from the window. "Come here. Look, there's a bloke in our yard!"

Rose and me bound across the bed and join Malcolm at the window, keeking out from behind the curtains. Sure enough there's a man in the shadow of our shed, looking up at the house. All we can see in the moonlight is the front of a white shirt beneath his jacket.

"It's Peter," whispers Rose. "He's followed me home. What does he think he's playing at?"

Just then the back door opens below us, Dad on his way out. Peter walks forward from the shed and starts talking to him. We can't see so well with the stone shelter in the way but Dad seems to be inviting him into the house.

"What's he gone and done that for?" pouts Rose as they both come inside. "He's the last person I want to see." But she can't stay sulking in our bedroom 'cause dad shouts "Rose?" at the foot of the stairs and she has to go down, with Mal and me sneaking behind her.

The good-looking young bloke stood in the middle of our living room is wearing a sharp suit, white shirt and tie. Only it's not Peter. It's Vince. Our Rose nearly faints when she sees him, and I'm sure that for a second all three of us believe we're staring at a ghost. Until he speaks.

"Hiya, Rose. You look smashing in that frock. What do you think o' this suit?"

Rose stands with her mouth open for a while, then says, "I... Have you been to the hospital?"

"Hospital. No, why? I've been to the Arcade."

"I thought you were going to Morpeth. In a van."

"I changed my mind, didn't I?" He shrugs. "A little birdie told me you were going dancing. So I thought I'd make the effort. I mean, I wasn't going to bust in on anybody. Just wanted to see you. Except you didn't turn up, like. I've been standing outside here for twenty minutes wondering whether it was too late to knock."

It's about the longest speech I've ever heard Vince make and the reason is nobody else is saying anything. Even after he shuts up there's silence, so he has to fill it again.

"So where were you, then?"

"Mayfair," says Rose quietly.

"The Mayfair? Ah." He looks at me and widens his eyes just a fraction. "The little birdie didn't tell me that bit. Was it good?"

"All right," says Rose. Then, "No, I like the Arcade better."

At last Mam says something. "Have you heard from your friends, Vince? Did they still go to Morpeth?"

"Suppose so, aye, just the four o' them. They weren't very chuffed wi' me though, tell you the truth. Prob'ly not speaking to us. But there you go. You gotta move on, haven't you? Can't be knocking about with single lads the rest of your life. No future in that, is there?"

While he's talking Rose has walked quietly into the middle of the room. She wraps her arms around him and cuddles him tight, burying herself into his neck and leaving makeup marks on his new shirt. He looks at me over her shoulder and I half-expect him to pull a funny face. But for once he doesn't.

The next time Vince has to wear his new suit is to go and see his mates buried. He asks Rose to go with him but it would mean her losing a day off work. "Remember, we've got some serious saving to do," she tells him, so he ends up going on his own.

That night we're just settling down for our tea, Rose still in her factory clothes, when there's a right rattle at the front door.

"Who can that be at this time?" says Mam, irritated. People we know would always use the back and generally just come in, so if there's a knock at the front door you can bet it's Jehovah's Witnesses or somebody else you don't want to talk to. I'm sent out of my chair and through the living room to find out who it can be. I open up and step back in shock. Filling the doorway is one side of a huge grey horse.

"Is your sister in?" comes a voice and I have to look way up to see Vince grinning with the sky behind him. He's riding bareback in his brand new suit, carrying a bunch of flowers.

"Rose!" I yell at the top of my voice. The mare gives a snort and tosses its head. "Sorry, Silver," says I, patting her.

Rose comes through into the passage and gasps at the sight of Vince and the horse on the step. Vince leans forward and presents her with the flowers like he's doing it to a roll of drums. Silver gets in on the act, turning to munch at the flowers so Rose has to snatch them away. She hands them to me then looks back at her boyfriend on the horse.

"You're daft as a brush, you."

"Fancy going for a ride?" he asks, reaching his hand down to her.

"You'll not catch me up there," she says, but not in the way she said it last time, and she takes his hand while I stand behind watching, holding her flowers like a bridesmaid at her wedding.

LOOKING ON

LOOKING ON

Babes

We're on Second Avenue, splashing past rows of colliery houses when Dad stops.

"Can you guess who used to live up that street?" he says, pointing.

He's not generally one for quizzes. Malcolm and me both look up at him, squinting in the rain. My brother's carrying his football boots round his neck with the laces tied together. Under his mac his legs are still caked with mud from the game at the Welfare. I've been watching and Dad's been helping to run the line, his big hankie getting more and more soaked so it's more like a dishcloth than a flag by the end.

"Beatrice Street. Do you not know?"

"Is it Bobby Charlton?" says our Mal, flicking a raindrop off his nose and leaving a brown streak there.

"Aye. Not long since he was kicking a ball in that back lane. His mam and dad's here yet. If we knocked on their door now they'd have us in and Cissie would be putting the kettle on."

But instead the three of us go back to our own house where Malcolm and me get the cigarette cards out on the hunt for Bobby Charlton. There he is in his red strip, older-looking than 20, smiling like somebody has just asked him to. On the back of the card the first thing it says under his name is *born Ashington, Northumberland* and I'm still surprised to see it written down even though I know it's true.

We riffle through the cards for the other Man United players and lay them down next to Bobby. There's Tommy Taylor, Eddie Colman, the captain Roger Byrne, Dennis Viollet, David Pegg. One player we're still hoping to collect is big Duncan Edwards who my dad reckons is even better than Charlton and maybe that's fair enough as he's been turning out for England since he was just 18 while Bobby hasn't got any England caps yet.

"You know what we should do when it stops raining?" says Malcolm while we're sorting out swaps on the kitchen table. "We should take the ball across to Beatrice Street and have a kick about."

"What for?"

"So we can always say we played football in Bobby Charlton's back lane."

It pours most of the afternoon and water's still draining down gullies by the time Malcolm and me start thumping a soggy caser between us at the back of Beatrice Street. At least the rain has meant nobody's strung a washing line across the way so we're not going to get some wife after us for mucking up her clean sheets off the ball.

In fact there's not a soul about so Malcolm drops further and further back to practise his long free kicks, keeping a wireless commentary on the go at the same time.

"And, would you believe it, Billy Wright is inviting young Bobby Charlton, in his first ever game for England, to take the free kick. Surely even Charlton can't beat the mighty Yashin from this distance."

The mighty Yashin, being me, waits in the middle of the lane while Charlton takes a huge run up and swings at the ball, slicing it high and wide onto a coalhouse roof and off into somebody's back yard.

We come together and stand looking at the red door our ball has bounced behind.

"Nip in and get it, youngun," says Malcolm. "It's your throw-in."

"Will I nick. You're the one wellied it, you can get it back."

Mal puts his hand on the sneck and pushes at the yard door but it doesn't budge. We stand looking at it a while longer.

"Maybe this is where the Charltons live," I say at last.

"How do you make that out, like?"

"I'm just thinking, the gate's the same red as Man U's. And maybe they've bolted it 'cause they're sick of people coming to ask about Bobby."

"You'd expect they'd chuck the ball back at least, if they're Charltons," says Malcolm, scuffing his foot against the brickwork.

"Prob'ly not in. They might be down Manchester to see him."

"You'll have to shin over the wall, then," goes Mal.

"Why me?"

"'Cause you're the lightest, aren't ya? Here, I'll give you a bunk up." He cups his hands like a stirrup for my foot.

As I'm scrabbling to get a fingerhold on top of the wall I hear the bolt being drawn back underneath. Mal springs away from the gate and I'm left dangling as a woman with a pinny on comes booling out into the lane.

"Get down from there, you little scamp," she hollers at me and grabs at my foot. I scrape down the wall and collapse in a heap at her feet.

"Please can we have our ball back?" says Malcolm in his polite voice while I sit nursing a graze on my knee.

"You're not from round here," she says. "Why don't you play at your own doors?"

I rock backwards to get a proper look at her. "Are you Bobby Charlton's mam?"

She laughs. "Oh, this is your game, is it, following in Bobby's footsteps?"

That's cheered her up. I'm just thinking she'll maybe invite us in for a cup of tea when she goes on, "Well, you're off target. The Charltons live yon side o' Beatrice Street. You're playing in the wrong back lane." She's still cackling about this as she steps back into her yard and rams the bolt to.

My brother and me wait hopefully for the ball to be lobbed back over the wall, but it hasn't showed by the time more rain starts up and we have to trail home in the gloom without it.

We've already missed the football results on Sports Report but Eamonn Andrews is on about the Busby Babes scoring five against Arsenal's four at Highbury. Nine goals altogether – it's like the games Roy of the Rovers plays in The Tiger but this is for real, with Bobby Charlton in the middle of it. He's scored, so has Edwards and Viollet, and Tommy Taylor's got two. Next week there's the second leg of the European Cup match. For once we forget Newcastle and become Man U fans.

Anyway it's OK to support the team in Europe since it's the same as shouting for England. Even Dad's caught up with it and we're all three glued to the wireless on Wednesday to hear what happens in Belgrade.

"Yes!" from Malcolm and his fist raised when Dennis Viollet puts us in the lead after just ninety seconds. "Get in, Bobby," and "Yes!" again when Charlton scores twice in two minutes. By halftime it's 5-1 on aggregate and the Babes seem a certainty for the semi-final.

Everything nearly goes pear-shaped in the second half. Snow is falling on the pitch and Harry Gregg's having real problems holding onto the shots from Red Star. *Three* goals he lets in and we're holding our breaths for the final whistle. When it comes at last the commentator is trying not to sound too excited, but you can tell he's chuffed. In our house it's all hell let loose.

The buzz is right round school next morning. Loads of kids have brought in their Man U cigarette cards and there's team formations laid out all over the yard at playtime. Malcolm's hogged our cards so when we're coming back into school I swipe them off him. Under the lid of my desk I'm flicking through the faces: Harry Gregg, Roger Byrne, Bobby Charlton...

"Are you listening, boy?"

"Eh?" I look up and suddenly it's all gone quiet. Mr Thain's staring at me and so are all the kids in the class.

"Sorry, sir." I'm trying to squeeze the cards into a neat pack under my desk without looking down.

"What you hiding there?"

"Nothing, sir."

"Don't you lie to me, boy."

He collects his strap from the front desk and in three strides he's down the aisle and grabbing my arm. That jerks the cards out of my hand and they scatter under my desk and around his shoes.

"Pick 'em up. Quickly!" and he towers over while I gather them in, then yanks me onto my toes so hard my head rattles the desk lid on the way.

"I'll have these," he says, snatching the cards. "And you..." He flicks my knuckles with his belt. We all know that signal. I stretch my hand out, palm up, and he thwacks it three times with the leather.

Mr Thain leaves me scrunched up nursing my hand under my arm while he drops the pile of cards and his strap onto his desk, then swings round to face the class.

"As I was saying, before I was so rudely interrupted…"

We're nearly finished last lesson when Maurice Pitt comes back in from his visit to the dentist with a scarf round his mouth like a bandit. I'm puzzling why he hasn't skived off home, same as anybody would this time of day never mind hurrying to his desk as if he can't wait to catch up on the Journey of Tea.

Instead of opening his book he pulls down his scarf and whispers urgently to Colin Ashburn in the seat next to him. Colin looks as if he doesn't believe what he's hearing, or maybe he can't make Maurice out with his fat lip. He quietly tears a page from the back of his notebook and pushes it across, watching over Mo's shoulder till he's finished writing.

Colin stares at the note, then at Maurice, then round at the class before he leans across the aisle to tug at Paul Miller's sleeve. As soon as he's got some attention Colin makes on he's studying the blackboard while he folds up the note and flips it sideways onto Miller's desk.

Whatever the message is it's creating a stir as it's passed from one lad to another and I'm right fidgety 'cause the closer it comes to me the more restless the class is becoming. I'll get crucified if Mr Thain cops us twice in one day, so I'm keeping one eye on him like a spuggie minding out for next door's cat.

He's still turned away chalking on the blackboard when Grant Stevens lobs the paper onto my desk and hisses, "Pass it on."

I pretend to be writing with one hand while I open the folds with the other and read the note. I don't notice that my pencil's stopped or that I'm pressing too hard on the page, till the tip snaps and brings me back to the room.

I glance around, seeing lads on my left whispering to each other and lads on my right saying nowt, watching me, waiting for their turn. I look down at the message again.

Man U plane has crashed whole team nearly dead

I keep reading the words, stupidly trying to work out if it means nearly the whole team is dead or they're all nearly dead, with doctors trying to save them the way they do in Emergency Ward 10. Something digs into my side and I turn. Clarky's poking me with his ruler and his mouth is going "pass it on" behind his hand, sort of loud but with no sound coming out, like he's drowning and crying for help. It's not just him, I feel as if the whole class is underwater with everything in slow motion. Only my mind is racing. All I can think of as the paper floats across to Clarky is, have Bobby's mam and dad been told?

By the time we're walking home it seems the whole world knows about the accident – even the lollipop lady was asking whether we'd heard – but there's all sorts of confusion about where it happened and who's alive and who's not.

"They'll all be killed," says Derek Nesbitt. "You don't get survivors with a plane crash. It's about a ten thousand foot drop."

"They never got up in the air," somebody else claims. "It happened on the ground at Munich airport. They slewed off the runway in the snow and hit a house or summat."

"What you on about, they weren't even coming from Munich. There were in Belgrade, dummy. Remember, Red Star Belgrade? Bloody idiot."

It's not until the six o' clock news that we get to hear properly about the plane stopping off for fuel at Munich and the pilot trying three times to take off in the bad weather. The third time the plane didn't lift off at the end of the runway. It just ploughed straight through the fence, hit two buildings and caught fire.

There's 21 killed. Seems Bobby's got out more or less OK, but Tommy Taylor's dead, so is Whelan, Jones, Colman, Pegg, Bent and Roger Byrne the skipper. Matt Busby's badly hurt in hospital, and dad reckons the way they're talking it'll not be long before he's a goner. Another one in a bad way is Duncan Edwards.

"Give us them cigarette cards over," says Malcolm to me. "I want to check who we've got again."

"Em, they're not here just now."

"What you on about? I lent you them at school."

"Yeah, but..." I can tell I'm going to be knacked for this. "They got confiscated. They're lying on Mr Thain's desk."

"Oh, you stupid..." I'm waiting for Malcolm to follow up with a clout, but instead he bursts into tears. "I was wanting to look at them cards. I was wanting to look at them," he cries and goes rushing upstairs. I've seen my brother cry before, but for once he doesn't seem to be putting it on. I don't follow him up. I sit, shrinking into the chair in front of the fire, and pick at the scab on my knee.

Saturday morning Malcolm's back at the Welfare playing for the school. Dad's been on fore shift so he's in bed but I'm there, standing for the minute's silence to remember the people who died at Munich. We win 3-1, with Mal scoring the second goal.

On our way home we pass the back row of Beatrice Street where the woman kept our ball, but we know it'll be a waste of time going to ask for it. At the end of the next block, Bobby's back row, we stop and look along. About halfway down there's a rare sight, a big silver car moving off in the other direction and a woman waving from a gate, facing away from us.

"I bet Bobby Charlton's in that car," shouts Malcolm. "Howay."

We run up the lane but by the time we're halfway the car has turned the corner and the woman's gone back into her house.

"I'm away to knock on them," says Mal.

I follow him into the woman's yard. "What you gonna say?"

"Dunno." He knocks on their back door. It's green, I notice, not Man U red. There's a man's voice from inside the house, then the woman who was waving at the car opens up for us. She's around Mam's age, fair-haired and for some reason I'm surprised she's wearing glasses.

"Hello, Mrs Charlton," goes our Malcolm. How does he know it's her? "We came to ask if Bobby's all right."

The man indoors calls out to her again.

"It's just a couple o' laddies, Bob," she shouts back.

Bob! Is Bobby Charlton inside the house? Then this bloke about fifty appears in the doorway behind the woman. Bob must be his dad's name as well.

He asks who we are and we tell him.

"Oh, I know your father," he says, like he was proud of it. "I used to go to the boxing wi' Frank."

"They've come asking about Bobby," says the woman, and for the first time I'm convinced this really is Cissie Charlton.

"Oh, he's ... fine," says Bobby's dad. "Got away with a bang on the head. He's OK, physically like."

"He'll be back playing in a week or two," says Mrs Charlton. "We've been very lucky, really. Here, come in a minute, I've something to show you."

And we go into the house, Bobby Charlton's house. The first thing I notice about the room she leads us into is how neat it all is, like her. Bobby's mam sits us down and disappears for a minute. While she's gone Malcolm nudges me and nods ever so slightly towards one corner of the room. Propped up there is one of them little banjos like George Formby plays. I'm wondering whose it might be when Mrs Charlton comes back in with what looks like a stamp album but turns out to be a scrapbook.

"I see you're a footballer," she says to Malcolm, who's holding his muddy boots by the laces an inch away from her clean carpet. "My brothers were professionals, and of course you know who my cousin is, don't you?"

"Jackie Milburn," says Malcolm as we make way for her to sit between us with her scrapbook.

"That's right. There's football in our blood, all from the Milburn side, naturally. Funny enough, *he's* always been more interested in the boxing, haven't you, pet?" Mr Charlton is by the hearth gazing into the fire but he looks up for a second when she speaks to him and smiles without saying anything.

"I've got scrapbooks for all of them, all the boys. This is Bobby's." She opens the first page. "That was his junior school team."

I can see Mal glancing sideways at me as we look at the same picture we've seen hanging in our own school corridor of eleven-year-old Bobby and his team mates sitting behind a cup, dressed in the identical football strip that my brother has on now under his coat.

For the next half hour Cissie takes us through the scrapbook of photos and pages cut from the newspapers, telling us how it was her that first taught the lads to kick a ball, how scouts from all the football clubs have been coming to the house ever since Bobby was our age, and how Manchester United was always going to be the one for him. When she reaches the first blank page in the book I notice there's a pile of loose cuttings, one with a picture of the aeroplane crash, that she mustn't have had time to sort out yet.

"Ee, I'd better let you away," she says at last. "Your mam will be wondering where you are."

As we get ready to go Mr Charlton, who's said nothing all this time, stands up and searches for something in a letter rack on the sideboard. Stuck in front of the rack is a folded paper with a printed crown between the words POST and OFFICE and TELEGRAM underneath.

"Do you fellers collect these?" he asks, holding out a few cigarette cards. We nod and he divides them between us, a couple each. "Tell Frankie I was asking after him," he says.

As we're walking away up Beatrice Street Malcolm's studying the cards Mr Charlton gave him. "I've got Ivor Allchurch and Ron Flowers. Who did you get?" I take the cards out of my pocket and puzzle over the picture of a player in a Leeds shirt. Malcolm glances across and says straight away, "John Charles. He's at Juventus now. Who else?"

I bring the next card out from behind John Charles. "Oh, you jammy bugger!" yells Mal. The face of Duncan Edwards is smiling up at us.

All through Monday, same as I did the day after the crash, I sit looking at our little stack of Man United cards next to the ink bottle on Mr Thain's desk. At four o' clock when we've sung Now the Day is Over and the class is filing out quietly I hang back, hoping that the teacher will remember he's still got my cards. But he just carries on with his marking and doesn't seem to notice I'm there. I have to go right up to his shoulder and give a pretend cough before he looks up.

"Yes?"

"Sir, I was just wondering whether I could have my cigarette cards back, please."

He glances at the pile on his desk, then fixes a stare at me, saying nothing. I take a deep breath.

"Only my dad was wanting to show them to Mr Charlton."

"What?"

"Mr Charlton senior, I mean. Bobby's dad. You see, my dad and him used to go boxing together and they're like good friends and that. Only my dad was telling him about the Manchester United cards what me and Malcolm collect and Mr Charlton was very interested and said he would like to see them, sir. That's the only reason I was asking."

Mr Thain taps his fingers on the desk and sighs. He looks again at the cards, then up at the ceiling. When he speaks it's as if the whole class is still there.

"You know, it amazes me. In fact, I find it quite incredible. The number of people in this town who know the Charltons, are related to the Charltons, are the best friends of the Charltons..."

He sighs again, reaches out to grab the pile and thrusts it at me. "Here. And if I catch you with these in school *once* more I'll rip 'em to pieces in front of your eyes."

"Yes, sir," and I'm away before he changes his mind.

Up in my bedroom I take Duncan Edwards from the toffee tin under the bed and place him on top of Bobby Charlton and the other Man U players. Then I put them all back in the tin and scratch *Busby Babes* on the lid with the point of a dart before I put it back under the bed.

The next time I see the face of Duncan Edwards it's on the front page of The Journal a couple of days after the team have started playing again and beaten Sheffield Wednesday 3-0 in a cup tie. The story is not about that game, though. It's saying how Duncan's just died in hospital from his injuries at Munich.

A few weeks later we're sitting having our tea when it comes on the wireless that Bobby's been called up for the England-Scotland game.

"That's good news, isn't it?" says Mam.

"Oh, it was bound to happen some time," Dad says, "But it makes you wonder how long Duncan Edwards and them would have kept him out if they'd lived. We'll never know."

"I know one thing," comes back Mam. "There's a woman in Ashington who'll be as proud as punch."

"Who, Cissie? You're not wrong there, like. Well, we're all proud of him, aren't we? Let's just hope he can make a good go of it now he's got his chance."

I can't help smiling, thinking of it now. Thinking about all the scrapbooks Cissie Charlton's going to need for Bobby.

Washed with Milk

The poshest thing we had in our house was what Mam always referred to as our *canteen* of cutlery. The word confused me for years because I knew my sister Rose ate her dinner in a canteen at work and that certainly wasn't posh. I couldn't imagine the factory lasses opening a long hinged box with silver crowns on the lid and unwrapping shiny knives, forks and spoons from tissue paper every time they sat down to eat their bait.

Nor could I imagine us doing it. In all my time at home the canteen of cutlery stayed in the sideboard drawer except for maybe once a year when Mam would perform a ritual on the dining table, washing and polishing every piece, not in the bustling way she normally did housework, but slowly and carefully unwrapping and cleaning and rewrapping each one separately as if she was preparing a row of miniature corpses for burial. I never once saw them set out in place for a meal. Mam always said they were being kept for *best*, for when we had *company*. Apparently whatever company we did have on the odd occasion never quite made the grade as far as Mam or that canteen of cutlery was concerned. We might have seen it in action the day Princess Margaret came to open Ashington Technical College but as it happens she never called round to ours.

It wasn't just the name that puzzled me – it was how this canteen of cutlery ever got to be part of the belongings in our house. I was told by more than one member of the family that Dad won it in a leek show. When I heard this I just looked out of our back window. Could they be talking about the same man who blithely let that garden straggle up to three feet high while his spade hung rusting from a nail in our shed from one July to the next? Maybe his leeks were in a plot out there, undiscovered by me, with the tall weeds protecting them against the worst of the weather so that when he came to lift them for the show he amazed all the hard-working gardeners who, not knowing the secret, had spent their year in a losing battle against the North East climate.

As usual it's our Malcolm who puts me right though I'll admit I'm not convinced at first when he says, "Dad doesn't grow leeks at all. He gets given 'em by Uncle Josh to put in the show."

I can easily believe the bit about Dad not growing the leeks. What I can't get my head around is this Uncle Josh. "What do you mean, Uncle Josh? We haven't even got an Uncle Josh."

"'Course we have. Auntie Ellen's husband."

"Auntie Ellen?" I know Auntie Ellen right enough. She's my dad's sister, lives in one of the end houses in Chestnut Street. Always has a sweet or a biscuit to give you. Very nice house as well, though there's a bit too much stuff in it for my liking. Take the front room, for instance. There's a three piece suite around a coffee table. Two china cabinets against the back wall. Why would anybody need one china cabinet, never mind two? Next to the hearth there's a fireside chair and a puffy. Sheepskin rug, flying ducks on the wall, companion set next to the fire ... but no husband that I've ever seen. I've always thought she lives there on her own.

"He's at the allotment every hour o' the day, that's why you never see him," explains Malcolm. "He's famous in Ashington, Uncle Josh, man. Been in the papers an' everything. He's the best leek grower round here bar none. You know all that furniture they've got in their house? Prizes, every stick of it. They pay for nowt."

Mal sounds pretty confident about all this, but I still have my doubts about the existence of Uncle Josh until I hear Dad say to Mam one Saturday morning in September, "I'm away ower to see how Josh is getting on with my blanchies," and I'm up like a dog begging for a walk.

"Can I go, Dad?"

They both stare like I'm Oliver asking for more. It's unheard of for me and Dad to go anywhere just the two of us. When he gets over the shock he says, "Get your coat, then. You'll have to walk back yoursel' though, mind. There's a bloke I need to see up the street later on." I know, same as Mam knows, what that means and it makes no odds to me. I can find my way home from anywhere in Ashington as well as Dad can find his way to the club.

One place I've never been, though, is the allotments back of Woodhorn Road. It's like a shanty town sprawling along the edge of the railway line. There's huts topped roughly with corrugated iron roofs, tiers of pigeon crees coated in whatever colours have come to hand from the remains of paint tins, odd constructions of bricks and window glass to make cold frames, uneven rows of fences and gates, some upright, some slanting, some with nailed-on boards or old doors on their sides...

The allotment we're headed for, even though it's one of the largest, is so neat among all this jumble and scrap that it seems tidied away almost out of sight. The first I see of Uncle Josh is a backside in a boiler suit as he's kneeling away from us, face among his plants. Dad has to call out "Aye-aye, Josh," before he realises we're there.

"Aye-aye, Frank. Long time no see," he says as he climbs to his feet. "Oh, you brung one o' the bairns along?" he adds, smiling down at me vaguely, as if he's having as much difficulty working out which one I am as I have placing him. He seems a nice enough chap and looks about the right fit for Auntie Ellen, but I'd swear I've never seen him before in my life.

"How's the leeks coming?" says Dad.

"Oh, canny, far as I can tell afore they get lifted. Here's yours yonder."

We spend the next few minutes staring down at a row of planted drain pipes with leaves showing out the top of them while Dad explores the mysteries of growing leeks. "Is it right you should piss on 'em?" he asks, with a guilty sideways glance at me as he says it.

"Not if you've got any sense," Uncle Josh comes back. "The uric acid could damage the stems. You hear that many daft recipes, man. Old wives' tales, mostly. Newcastle Brown Ale's a common one. Waste of time."

"Waste o' good beer," agrees Dad. "Another one I heard about is dried cattle blood."

"I told you what Sammy Cole did last year?"

"No."

"That's Sam's allotment ower the way, look," says Uncle Josh, pointing it out. "See that big water butt?"

"Aye."

"He only went an' put a dead dog in there. Steeped it in for I don't know how long. Place was honkin', man. Then he irrigated his leeks with it."

I stare across at the water barrel, then back at Uncle Josh. He had to be joking, surely. But his face is straight as he stands contemplating Sammy Cole's allotment. After a pause he says, "He'll not be doing that again, like."

"Ah, did the health board catch up with 'im?" asks Dad.

"Not that," says Uncle Josh. "His leeks never got placed in any show last year. Not a one. Waste of time." He prods at the soil and goes on. "No, there's only one recipe for cultivatin' leeks that seems to work, other than a lot o' hard graft, that is."

"What's that?"

"Sheep shit," says Uncle Josh emphatically.

"Really?"

"Oh, aye. I'm often up Newbiggin Moor wi' me pail and shovel. Duggie's farm, an' all. Canna' get enough of it. Very good manure, sheep's droppings."

With that piece of advice to ruminate on, and having arranged to pick up his show leeks in a fortnight, Dad gets ready to leave. But as I'm following him to the gate Uncle Josh calls out, "You'll not have such a thing as a little tent, have you, youngun?"

"No, why?"

"I was just wanting to borrow one for a short while."

"S'pose I could ask my mate Alan Chisholm. He's in the cubs."

"Oh, cubs, is he?" comes Uncle Josh. "They'll have their Harvest Festival coming up. Tell him if he can get me the lend of a tent till a week on Friday, I'll give them a whole barrow-load o' fruit and veg to hand out to the old folk."

This bribe works a treat and a couple of days later me and Chiz turn up with a two-man khaki scout tent. Straight away Uncle Josh gets us to help him put it up on a patch of ground he's cleared specially at the bottom of the allotment.

"You're not camping out here, are you, Uncle Josh?" says I, spinning a finger at the side of my head for Alan's benefit while my uncle is in the tent rolling out the groundsheet.

"Why aye," he says, emerging. "Where did you think I was going, Druridge Bay? I'll not be moving from this spot for the next ten days."

"What for?"

"To keep an eye on the leeks, of course. It's less than a fortnight to the biggest show of the year. We don't want them walkin'."

Now I'm sure he's crackers. "How can leeks start walking? They're plants. They're stuck in the ground."

It's his turn to look at me as if I'm an idiot. "I mean we don't want them pinched," he says. "Look, the show stewards have to come along and stamp the leeks with a number that proves they're mine. Your dad'll get the ones in his plot stamped with a different number. But until that happens it's been known for some buggers to sneak up in the night, lift somebody else's leeks and transplant them in their allotment, pass 'em off as their own."

"They'll do that just to win a prize in a leek show?"

"They'll do worse than that, bonnie lad, specially these days. There's a Blyth allotment had every leek slashed a couple o' days before they were due to show. I've seen prize specimens destroyed where somebody's poured Domestos on them. Air guns they use, sometimes. Oh, you'd be surprised at what some people get up to in the world of leeks."

So says Uncle Josh as he prepares to spend the best part of the next fortnight under canvas in his allotment next to the railway line.

Friday week my dad gets a big towel out the airing cupboard, rolls it up under his arm and sets off again for Uncle Josh's allotment. Me and Chiz are in tow to help take the tent down and carry it back to the scout hut. I might have guessed though that Uncle Josh has already got everything sorted. As we troop through his gate we see him sitting cross-legged on a sack, smoking his pipe like a Red Indian chief at peace. On one side of him is the tent neatly packed up. In front, laid out on a mat as if they were scalps on display, is a set of three healthy blanch leeks.

"I've got some grand ones for you here, Frank," he says as we walk up the path. Dad takes his towel from under his arm and spreads it next to the mat ready to transfer the leeks while Uncle Josh bends over to supervise the operation. Make them two women and we could be looking at a delivery room.

"I've cleaned the debris off and given them a trim," says Josh. "Make sure you bathe them carefully when you get home. If you've got a baby comb you can put that gently through the roots, just a stroke, like." He wraps the towel lovingly over his three charges and tenderly lifts them up for Dad to cradle in his arms.

"How's your set looking?" Dad asks and Uncle Josh smiles, nodding slightly.

"Oh, they're real beauties. I'm very pleased with them, very pleased. We should both do well tomorrow, Frank. What's been your best placing to date?"

"Fifth."

"You might improve on that. If I was a betting man I'd say you would. But we'll see tomorrow, eh?"

When I come home from dropping the tent off at the scout hut, Dad's already in the back end titivating up his leeks so I hang around for a bit to watch what's going on.

"Look and see if there's any milk left in that pantry, son," he says over his shoulder while he drains some dirty water out the sink.

There's nearly a full bottle keeping cold on the floor so I hand it over to Dad who sniffs at it then dives into the cupboard under the sink for Mam's big mixing bowl. He pours all the milk into the bowl and sticks the empty bottle on the kitchen window-sill. "Where's your mam keep her pastry brush?" he says next.

I have to negotiate around him to get into the drawer for the brush. He cups his left hand round the back of one leek to lift it up while he dips the brush in the bowl of milk with his right. Then he carefully brushes the white stem like he's adding some final touches to a work of art.

"What you doing that for, Dad?"

"Feller in the club told us this is the way to get a nice soft finish on your leeks. Makes sense to me." He dips in the milk again and I watch him as he raises his brush to the stem, his little finger sticking up as delicate as Michelangelo or a genteel old lady come for tea. Dad's really caught the leek show bug.

Saturday morning he's up bright and early as it's a fair walk from ours to the White House Social Club and anybody who's late for staging gets disqualified. I feel I'm part of this now so I get up early as well to watch him go. I have to eat Weetabix with butter on for my breakfast since the milkman hasn't been yet and Dad used up all we had last night. He takes his tea without so he's not bothered.

All the entries have to be set up and everybody out of the hall by ten at the latest, then the judges are on their own with the leeks and onions for two hours. I can't wait until half past twelve when the show opens and we can go and see who's won all the prizes. I have a good feeling about this.

On the rare times Mam goes out anywhere other than the shops she always takes an age getting ready. By the time we get to the White House we're well back in the queue. Dad's nowhere to be seen but it's not hard to guess he'll be in the bar where me and Malcolm are not supposed to go, so just the three of us make our way into the room where the show is.

Mam takes as much interest in the prizes that's on display in the middle of the hall as she does in the entries laid out on tables along the sides, but I'm keen to find out the results so I'm constantly tugging at her sleeve to keep up with the people snaking round clockwise. It's Malcolm, though, who spots the first triumph for the family. "Look, Uncle Josh has won summat for his onions."

Sure enough there's a tidy collection of onions with a card announcing 1st J. Ede next to the pink cloakroom ticket showing the blind entry number. That'll please Uncle Josh, but I understand enough by now to realise what he has his heart set on is the big one. Champion leek.

Next after the onions is the pot leeks. Though I know Dad hasn't got any entries in this class I'm surprised not to see Uncle Josh's name anywhere among the cards marking prize-winners and commendations. Maybe he's been concentrating on his blanchies and not bothered entering pot leeks.

Finally on the far side of the hall we see where the blanch leek entries are laid out. My brother and me are craning our necks trying to see past the people in front of us, looking for the all-important cards. We get our eyes on the same one together and Mal nearly knocks me over with his excited bear hug as I turn back to yell at Mam, "Third! Dad's won third prize!"

Mam puts on a delighted expression then peers over her right shoulder trying to spot third prize on the central display, but I hurry her on to where people are bunching up to stare at one of the entries further along the aisle. On the way Malcolm points out the runner-up. "2nd. R. Dunning. Never heard of him," as if he's been going to leek shows for years.

I have to worm my way through a crowd of grown-ups, leaving Malcom and Mam behind, to get to the entry that's attracting all the attention. Three leeks stretched out like they're trying to get the sun on their long white legs. Tidy leaves, trim beards, all dressed up to win. It's just as the card alongside says, Best in Show, and then the name ... S. Cole.

S. Cole. Sammy Cole. But what about Uncle Josh? He said his were beauties, and he should know. I've missed summat somewhere. He's got to have won a prize. Where's the card with *his* name on?

Malcolm's arm comes through bodies and sucks me out of the crowd. "Well?" he says. "Has he won it? Is it Uncle Josh?"

"It's Sammy Cole," I say in a daze, my mind still inside a water butt with a mangey, smelly dog floating dead.

We wander over to where Mam is standing by the prizes on display. "Third prize is a man's suit from the Co-op," she says, disappointed, but only runner-up in disappointment next to me. Or so I reckon until I come across Uncle Josh sitting on the steps at the front of the club in a suit he must have earned in some other leek show. He's the winner in the disappointment stakes by a country mile.

"Slashed!" he's saying into an empty glass between his knees. "Blanch leeks. Pot leeks. Butchered by some butcherin' bastard. They might as well have had me fucking onions and be done with it, pardon my French," he adds, looking unsteadily up at Mam. I get the idea Uncle Josh doesn't drink very often.

"But ... they were all right last night," I'm saying as my dad pushes through the swing doors with two full glasses. "That's what you camped out for."

"Might as well have gone home to wor lass," moans Josh. "Waste o' fu... flamin' time."

"It's been done here. Right here in the club," Dad explains to us as Uncle Josh has another go at drowning his sorrows. "We'd got all set out sweet as you like. They looked fantastic. I was pleased wi' mine, but Josh's leeks..."

"Perfect," from Uncle Josh, talking to his beer.

"We heard nowt until the judges was finished. 'Course they didn't know until the end whose leeks had been got at."

"Got at?" says Mam.

"Razor job," says Dad. "All six of Josh's leeks. It'll have taken seconds. Just a matter of somebody staying behind at the end of the set-up. Somebody who knew what they were doing. Whose leeks was whose..."

"I know who," says Uncle Josh.

"You're just surmisin', Josh," says Dad.

"I know who," Uncle Josh repeats. "I could smell him on my leeks. Dead dog's...eye." He tails off.

"Aye, well," says Dad, then to Mam, "I've offered him my new suit but he won't take it."

"I don't want your suit," says Josh. "It's not about suits. Or suites. Or fuckin' china cabinets. Tell you what though, Frank. I'm finished with this. As far as I'm concerned, that's it. It's over. I'm finished." And he sounds so deep and so empty I feel that he truly means it.

Except the very next weekend, when me and Chiz roll up to his allotment with a barrow, collecting for the Harvest Festival, we find him laying out three freshly dug leeks on his mat.

"What's these for, Uncle Josh?"

"Oh, them's for the show at the Fell 'Em Doon, son. It's the last one of the season. I've got a canny chance with these, I would say."

"Oh aye, you'll win with them all right."

"Never say die, eh?" he says, winking. And as we're leaving with the barrow full of fruit and veg he calls out, "Did your mam make some nice broth with them leeks of your dad's?"

"Oh aye. Lovely, Uncle Josh."

"Champion. That's what they're for at the end of the day, you know. There's a lot forget that. You enjoyed your broth, then?"

"Smashing thanks yeah."

Of course I haven't the heart to tell him how I had to put my spoon down after just one mouthful of leek broth on Sunday night, because all I could think about was sheep's droppings.

Fair Fight

Hughie Jakes was famous round our way long before the rest of Ashington got to know and love him. It's true that he did a few scary things while he was in what according to his birth certificate would be his teenage years – like chopping up our tortoise convinced it was an alien from outer space when it crawled through into their back garden, and trying one Easter to crucify his sister Doreen on the side of their shed so his mam had to come screaming out of the house to grab the hammer and nails off him – but once he was older he seemed to get a better grip on the rights and wrongs of life so never really gave any of us who knew him much cause to worry.

I say *once he was older*. You need to understand that Hughie Jakes had a year or two even on our Eddie, but he was still playing in the streets when I was seven and he wasn't far short of twenty-one. There was one thing he was absolutely brilliant at, and that was playing the part of drum major in front of an imaginary jazz band.

I suppose Hughie's mam must have taken him at one time or another to see an Ashington carnival parade. In between the floats a wave of juvenile jazz bands such as the Melody Makers or the Gay Geordies would crash down Station Road rattling on snare drums, clicking their sticks or wailing into kazoos.

Always in front of the band would be one of the older girls in a skimpy skirt and white boots, twirling and throwing a baton with what looked like a silver door knob on the end. Sometimes this lass in front would stretch her baton out to the side as a signal for her band to turn a corner, and occasionally she would blow a whistle to get them to march on the spot, or even stop playing if we were lucky.

Hughie loved all that. I guess he dreamed about being in front of one of these bands 'cause he would spend hour after hour marching up and down our street with a plastic whistle from a Christmas cracker in his mouth, spinning the handle of a sweeping brush round his fingers, throwing it up in the air and catching it when it came down again. Usually he'd have his sister acting out the rest of the band and sometimes we'd fall in as well for a laugh while big Hughie marched in front, bossing us all with his hand signals and whistles.

The amazing thing is that this overgrown kid who couldn't make head nor tail of a reading book and couldn't kick a football in front of him, never mind try anything more complicated like riding a bike, didn't once miss a beat on his march and never dropped a catch supposing he threw that broom handle twenty foot in the air.

Hughie grew like a cuckoo. Eventually his mam had to try and prise him out of the nest, at least for part of the day, and she did it by finding him work of a sort. She replaced his broom handle with a shovel and managed to persuade a few of the neighbours to let him put their loose coals in after the wagons dropped the loads pitmen were allowed every other week. Maybe people let him do it out of sympathy at first, but Hughie had found another thing he was good at and pretty soon a lot of people were after his services 'cause a tanner was a bargain for the quick, tidy job he did.

That was how the rest of Ashington came to know Hughie. He was as proud of that shovel as he had been of his baton and he would parade up and down the rows with it over his shoulder, following the coal wagon on its rounds. He would never have the nous to go and knock on anybody's door and ask to put their coals in, but once word got round people would look out for him so he was never short of a job or a cup of tea and maybe a Penguin biscuit or a Wagon Wheel for his break.

Malcolm and me were more than happy when Mam set Hughie on putting our coals in, unless we really needed cash for ourselves, then we'd try to persuade her to give us the job instead. We were even prepared to undercut poor Hughie if we were desperate.

That was the case when the shows came to People's Park. Through shovelling coal plus other jobs blagged and messages run, the pair of us managed to scrape together about four bob each in the days leading up to this particular Whit weekend.

"The thing to do," says Malcolm, taking charge as we pick our way through the travellers' caravans towards the lights and the music of the shows, "is to have a proper look at what's what first before we spend a penny, then we can choose what we'd like to go on before we run out o' dosh."

A sensible plan, and one that flies straight out of our heads as soon as we take in the burnt-sweet smell of toffee apples and see how easy it is to win a coconut just by lobbing a wooden ball into a tin pail or sticking darts into three separate playing cards.

"They've blunted them on purpose. I'm bringin' my own next time," Malcolm's moaning twenty minutes later when we're down to two-and-eight between us and no prizes to show from all the games we've tried. "Thieving gyppo," he mutters low enough to go unnoticed by the bloke who pointed out the No Fallen Darts Returned sign at the latest stall.

At least we've saved money by not going to see Hairy Mary and her Test Tube Baby. Derek Nesbitt sneaked under the back of the tent and he's tipped us the wink that the baby's a plastic doll in a glass tube and Hairy Mary is just a miserable little monkey chained to a table in the middle of the marquee.

Nez takes us along to the Roll a Penny where he's figured out an easy way to win some money back. He stations Malcolm and me round one side of the stall to roll pennies down the chutes over the numbered squares while he waits on the opposite side. There's a mesh right round to stop you placing the pennies by hand but Nez reckons he can get into the space between the mesh and the board underneath. He just needs us to distract the wife who is standing inside the circle watching over the games. When she turns away from him to pick our coins off the board Nez carefully pushes a penny with his finger under the mesh, aiming to place it right in the middle of a square with the number 4 printed on it.

It works. The wife swivels around to his side and casually skims four pennies from the pile in her hand across the board and under the grille to Nez. We dive into our pockets for more pennies to roll while Nez waits for the woman to turn her back on him again.

As she swoops down on our losing coins Nez pokes his fingers through the space under the grille. Maybe she already has him sussed or maybe she follows our eyes, I don't know, but just as he's stretching to guide another penny into the square she spins round and lunges forward, grabbing his finger ends.

"Ow, get off me hand!"

"You sneaky wee thief," she growls at him through the mesh. "Give us them coins back or I'll snap your bones."

She keeps tight hold till Nez has shunted all four pennies through to her side of the grille with his free hand then lets go, snarling, "Get out of it, you're barred." She turns on us, "And you!" as we sneak off into the crowd.

We leave Derek Nesbitt to his own devices after that, but his bright idea has wasted more of our cash and we're seriously short of funds now.

"As long as we've got enough for a turn on the Waltzer," says Mal. The big ride in the middle of the fairground is the centre of attraction. It has round cars on wheels that bob up and down like boats in a storm while hard men, who look as if they've come from working on an oily engine, stand with their legs apart, riding the waves easy and looking at nobody. Every so often they might trouble themselves to spin the cars with a shove to make the girls inside throw their heads back and scream up at the coloured light bulbs. Ninepence a go, single riders pay double.

We have to skirt round the outside of the stalls to steer clear of the Roll a Penny woman on our way to the Waltzer, which is how we find ourselves in among a crowd of folk staring up at one of the big booths making up the back line of the shows. This booth has two giant pictures of boxers painted on boards either side of a dark red curtain. One of the pictures is definitely supposed to be Freddie Mills, the other one is harder to guess - maybe Randolph Turpin wearing his Lonsdale Belt.

Lined up on a platform in front of the curtain there's three real-life fighters looking much more used and beaten up than the ones in the pictures. They're all in threadbare dressing gowns with dirty towels round their shoulders and wearing brown leather boxing gloves that look as if they've done even more rounds than these three have. Beside them is a bloke who reminds me of the comedian Arthur Askey in a black suit too tight for him, holding a microphone. There's wooden steps leading up to the platform and this short guy keeps sweeping his free arm like he's trying to draw the crowd up the steps.

"Come on, you young men out there. Who is going to be brave enough to take one of our champions on?" Another sweep of his left arm. His seam could split any second. He gets his eye on a couple of lads supping out of Brown Ale bottles near the front.

"How about you fine gents?" They look vaguely up at him, spluttering their beer and jostling each other. "Are you going to show the girls what you're made of?" There's a wolf whistle from somewhere in the crowd. "Listen, here's what I'm going to do for you. I'm not even asking you to knock my man out. If you can survive three rounds, just three short three-minute rounds, I'm going to *give* you, not one, not two, three, or four, but five, *five* pounds sterling for your efforts."

He counts on his fingers till the end of his spiel, then he reaches into his inside pocket, risking his seam again, and produces a five pound note that he waves towards the likely pair. They dilly-dally for a few seconds, eyeing up the opposition, but soon enough they take the bait and straggle up the steps to clapping and some banter from their pals in the crowd.

"Well done, lads," says the short bloke, taking their bottles away for safety and parking them behind a board. "Now, we only need one more volunteer and we're ready to get the show under way. Who else wants to earn five pounds for just nine minutes' work?"

There's movement behind us as people make way for somebody coming through. A murmur bubbles under then erupts in one massive cheer as a heavy figure climbs to the platform and turns round with a sloppy grin to face his adoring public.

"It's Hughie! Hughie Jakes!" yells Mal, catching the thrill of the crowd.

"What's *he* doing here?"

"He'll have followed the jazz bands down to the park. Hey, Hughie! Hughie, man!"

The MC must be wondering what all the excitement is about. Hughie is the most unlikely looking hero. What with his basin haircut, unshaven chin and his vest smeared with coal dust under his baggy jacket he nearly makes the fairground fighters look smart by comparison. But the short guy doesn't care what Hughie looks like, he can smell money.

From behind the curtain he produces a big leather satchel the same as our rent man has when he comes round the doors. He slings the long strap over one shoulder and starts to hustle for paying customers.

"Step right up, ladies and gentlemen, for the *big* show of the day. You'll see all three bouts for just one shilling piece. Just one bob for a ringside view right through these curtains. See your local lads make a name for themselves. Step right up, thank you, make way your way through the curtains there if you would. Don't push, there's plenty of room for all. Queue here, thank you kindly. Have your shillings ready, *please*."

As he's talking and selling, the three pro fighters double up as bouncers, guarding the entrance so nobody sneaks through the curtain without paying. A long queue forms by the steps. Hughie is obviously the star attraction. Some in the queue stretch across to shake his big paw as they reach the platform, others wish him luck or give him the thumbs up sign.

"Ah, we've got to see this," goes Mal.

"It's a bob each though, but. We'll have nowt left for the Waltzer."

"It's once in a lifetime, innit, watching big Hughie fight. The Waltzer'll be back next year."

So we join on the end of the queue to hand our shillings over, wave at Hughie and step through the red curtain into the big fight arena.

The grubby canvas tent and bare lighting behind the curtain may not be as glamorous as a circus big top but our excitement makes up for that. The atmosphere is electric. The problem for kids like us though is there's no seats in the place and already the crowd is standing six or seven rows deep around the boxing ring in the middle of the tent. Malcolm takes the lead trying to burrow a way through and burns his cheek on somebody's lighted fag.

"Ow!" he yelps, and the bloke looks down.

"Watch where you're going, son."

"I'm just trying to get an' see summat. Me an' my brother's spent all we've got on this an' we canna get a look in."

"Fair dos." The bloke parks his tab in one corner of his mouth and gives a lopsided warning, "Couple o' younguns coming ower." He stoops to pick Malcolm up and hands him over the heads of the people in front. Somebody grabs him and he disappears, then it's my turn. We're like barrels on the rapids, tumbling down to the front, but we're set down gently enough at the ringside and we couldn't have a better view.

Once everybody's packed into the place the bloke who looks like Arthur Askey climbs into the centre of the ring with his microphone. He's still carrying his satchel on his shoulder, not trusting anybody else with his money.

"Ladies and gentlemen, please be upstanding for our first two gladiators of the ring."

We're already upstanding so we make up for it by clapping and whistling while the fighters come through the ropes to get to their stools. The pro is rigged out in full boxing gear but other than the jacket his mate is holding for him, the lad from Ashington is still dressed in his ordinary clothes, plus a pair of oversized boxing gloves. He looks as pale as his shirt.

"Ladies and gentlemen, in the blue corner I give you Jolting Joe Walton from Preston in Lancashire." There's a hiss from the audience and as Jolting Joe scowls at them I notice he has a gum shield in place.

"And in the red corner our plucky challenger from Ashington, Nobby Longstaff."

Nobby half lifts a glove as the crowd cheer and he grins nervously at his pal in the corner. No gum shield.

Arthur Askey picks up a handbell from the far side of the ropes. "Seconds out, round one."

Jolting Joe charges so quick across the ring that Nobby stumbles back into the stool that his mate is trying to move out of the way and he goes sprawling onto the canvas before a punch is thrown. The MC turns ref, rushing across for the count while Joe waits to land one on Nobby as soon as he gets up.

"Get back in your corner!" some in the crowd are yelling, but both Joe and the ref ignore them. Nobby beetles around the ring on all fours and scrambles to his feet in the opposite corner, covering his head with his forearms. Joe hits him in the belly with his left then meets his chin on the way down with a right upper cut. Nobby snaps backwards and stretches full length on the canvas.

While Nobby's friend tries to revive him, dipping his fingers in a bucket and flicking water on his face through the ropes, the ref stands over the body, counting quickly up to ten, then he gives him the *kaput* sign and lifts Joe's lethal right glove high in the air.

"The *win-ner*, by a knockout in the first round, Jolting Joe *Wal-ton*."

There's boos all round the tent from people who had expected the fight to last more than thirty seconds, and the booing gets worse when Nobby's marrer drags his mate out the ring and tells Arthur Askey he can stuff his five pounds, there's no way *he's* risking his life in there. As they haul themselves off through the crowd the MC grabs the mike and cuts through the noise.

"Unfortunately, folks, our second challenger has withdrawn. Is there any gentleman in the audience who would be prepared to take his place?" He pauses and looks around in a stagey way like Ben Turpin used to in the silent pictures and every bloke he gets his eye on shuts up in case he accuses them of volunteering. When he's got quiet in the tent he brings the mike to his mouth again. "In that case I regret to announce *no contest* for the second bout. Ladies and gentlemen, please be upstanding to greet our gladiators on *top* of the *bill*."

Everybody brightens up when they see Hughie making his way to the ring. Somebody's put gloves on his mitts without even taking his jacket off. He's heading for the corner next to us and to be honest he smells a bit whiffy as he pulls himself up through the ropes, but Mal and me cheer him on more than anybody in the tent as he sort of belongs to us, living so close.

"Ladies and gentlemen, in the blue corner we bring you Sherwood Forest's most notorious outlaw, Mike Merryman." The crowd takes a rise out of this bloke since he walks in wearing a silly Robin Hood hat to match his green shorts, but when he throws it down in his corner and turns our way he becomes an evil bald-headed Turk the likes of which you always see guarding Mr Big.

Our Hughie doesn't look worried by him. He's taking more interest in the handbell that's parked just outside the ropes to signal the start of the rounds. He reaches through and lifts it up in his glove to inspect it just as the MC is saying, "And in the red corner your local favourite, Hughie Jakes."

There's another great cheer around the tent and Hughie acknowledges it by lifting the bell over his head and clanging it to add to the noise. This confuses the pro, who rushes out to start the fight while Hughie's still ringing, smacking him hard in the chest.

"Hoi!" goes Hughie, wheeling his arm round to defend himself. Merryman ducks but the edge of the bell glances his bonce, and he retreats to his corner cradling his head then looking at the inside of his forearm for signs of blood. The ref grabs Hughie's wrist to calm him down and ease the bell away from him. He picks up the mike and, pointing to Hughie, declares "First public warning" while we fill the air with boos against the decision.

The fight gets underway properly now. Mike Merryman starts prowling round his man, sizing him up, while Hughie stands quite content in the centre of the ring, letting his arms dangle loosely, enjoying the feel and weight of his gloves.

"Howay, Hughie, get stuck in!" somebody calls out. Hughie waves at the sound of his name just as if he's strolling along our street, and Merryman takes his chance. He darts in on Hughie's left and jabs him twice in the cheek. Hughie looks astonished and for a second his face crumples to cry. His bottom lip juts out, but then he sets his chin and trundles after Merryman with an offended look in his eyes.

With his arms out wide as a windmill Hughie traps Merryman in a corner where he swings at him, connecting first with his shoulder, then his head, then his body. The pro sinks down on one knee and the ref steps in to half-push, half-soothe Hughie away as the crowd swear and complain.

Merryman picks himself up without a count and protects himself at the referee's back, unscrambling his brains while the short bloke makes on to be giving Hughie a lecture.

As soon as the ref steps away Merryman springs another surprise attack, lunging his head forward into Hughie's face. Our man thumps onto the bald skull like he's banging his fist hard on a table. Merryman grabs onto him as he's going down and for a few seconds the pair of them dance around the ring for all the world as if they're two drunks at a wedding with the crowd laughing and egging them on.

After a couple of turns Hughie props his partner upright and taps him on both arms in a consoling sort of way. Merryman doesn't quite know what to make of this and wanders back to his corner. The ref isn't sure either so he rings the bell for the end of the round.

While he's waiting on his stool for round two, taking a swig of water from the bucket, Hughie gets his eye on Malcolm and me and gives us a beaming smile.

"Stick one on 'im, Hughie," yells Mal.

"Wha'?" goes Hughie, poking his head right out through the ropes towards us, straining to hear. I can't help thinking about that Hunchback of Notre Dame film.

"I said, stick one on the bugger," shouts Malcolm, pointing at the other bloke and punching his fist in the air. "For Ashington."

Hughie grins and nods. As soon as the bell rings for the second round he does his jazz band march across to the opposite corner and aims a mighty clout at Merryman, who swerves out of the way from the hips. Hughie follows up with another wild throw and cracks him on the back of the head, sending him to the floor. While the ref leaps across to navigate Hughie into a neutral corner the crowd does the other part of his job, chanting the count in full chorus.

On eight Merryman staggers to his feet. Hughie comes swinging at him again, his arms and elbows that high you'd think there was an invisible hula hoop spinning round his waist. Merryman ducks below where the hoop would be and charges sideways like a wrestler, upending Hughie who crashes heavily. We all groan for him then let off a bombardment of boos and hisses, drowning out the ref's counting over poor Hughie.

Our hero's not finished yet, though. All Merryman has done to him is get his dander up. Hughie lifts himself onto his backside for a couple of beats, looking to see where Merryman's hiding, then he's up and after him, flailing his fists and growling, "Oy, y' bugger. Stick one on y' bugger." Pro or not, the outlaw from Sherwood Forest is reduced to dodging all round the ring, on the run from the lad with the coal shovel swing.

We're getting dizzy watching, but not as dizzy as Merryman when he finally catches one full in the face. He totters and Hughie smacks him again with a beauty, making his gum shield fly out with a gobful of spit and blood over a bloke stood next to us in the front row. "Shite!" he goes, flicking at the mess on his coat. "Gobshite!" pipes up our Malcolm, and "Gobshite!" again to me, pleased with himself.

When we turn our attention back to the ring we see that the ref's trying to break things up, heaving Hughie away, with Mike Merryman sprawled against the ropes. He pulls our man by the sleeve of his jacket to the corner where the handbell is and stretches down for it. He rings the bell vigorously in Hughie's face as if he's trying to snap him out of his mood while a buzz starts up in the crowd.

"It's all over," announces Mal, nudging me. "Technical Knockout."

Still holding on to Hughie the ref exchanges the bell for the microphone. He's sweating as he looks around, as if he's been in the fight himself, then he raises his hand for silence and speaks to the mike.

"Ladies and gentlemen," he says. "I'm sure that those of you who follow boxing can understand why I've had to stop this fight."

Malcolm nods at me knowingly, some in the crowd are muttering "TKO" and others are just generally congratulating themselves. The Arthur Askey character goes on.

"It's obvious that this lad here," tugging Hughie by his sleeve, "has never boxed before, has no idea about boxing, though he's got a good heart. I think you'll agree he's got a good heart."

And we all find ourselves nodding and clapping Hughie for his good heart while he grins broadly and Mike Merryman slips out of the ring and through to the back of the tent. Arthur Askey reaches up to pat Hughie on his shoulder then brings the mike to his lips again.

"But, having no idea about boxing, it's obvious this lad was going to do serious damage to himself. Serious damage. And I can't allow that in my emporium. I have certain responsibilities, legal responsibilities, which I'm sure you'll all understand."

I'm not sure many people have understood, judging by the puzzled looks they're giving each other now.

"So as you'll understand and appreciate I had to stop the fight before this poor lad did serious hurt to himself or had serious hurt to him done by others. Both ways I'm responsible, it goes without saying. But here's what

I'm going to do for you, Hugh, for your good heart and your efforts today..." He pats Hughie on the chest like he's a horse, then he searches in his leather satchel and brings out a couple of notes. (I was half-expecting sugar lumps.) "Even though you didn't make it through all three rounds as the rules require, I'm going to give you these two pound notes in recognition of your courage in facing my boy this afternoon. So please give him a big hand, folks, your own *Hughie Jakes.*"

With that he ceremoniously tucks the money into Hughie's top pocket. Hughie is delighted, lifting his gloves above his head like a winner. A few in the tent break into applause but the anger swells up as different sections of the crowd start to cotton on to the trick that's been played.

"Cheat!" somebody shouts out.

"Give him his fiver," another one goes.

While Arthur Askey is stripping Hughie of his boxing gloves the booing starts, then a slow handclap that gets louder and louder, especially when Hughie joins in, clapping and dancing in the middle of the ring. People in the crowd press forward, pushing Malcolm and me right up under the ropes, and pretty soon Arthur's looking for his bouncers.

"Joe! Mikey!" But they're nowhere to be seen. He grabs hold of Hughie, pushing him on ahead to the corner where we are. "Get back, let the lad through here."

A way opens for Hughie, with some in the crowd patting his back as he climbs out of the ring and through to the exit. The short bloke tries to follow but as he's clambering through the ropes one joker grabs at his heel and he goes arse over tip in the air. His leather satchel tips up with him, showering us with silver and bronze coins, just like a wedding car scramble.

I've never seen an old man move as fast as Arthur trying to gather his money in. As soon as he hits the deck he's up like a cat, foraging through the grass and under the boxing ring for lost coins. But he's got plenty of competition. It seems like half the tent are down on their knees searching, including Malcolm and me. We disappear quick enough when Jolting Joe Walton emerges from the back of the tent and looses off a fire extinguisher over the lot of us. Joe's boss gets as much of it as anybody but whether that was an accident I couldn't tell you.

I'm already quizzing Malcolm while we're still running from the spray. "Have we got enough for the Waltzer?"

"Why aye," he comes back. "Enough for two and three turns."

And this time we make sure we head straight to it, no distractions. There's a ride already on the go and we have to wait with a crowd of others, preparing to dash for a car as soon as the Waltzer slows down. We stand on the boards listening to The Coasters singing Charlie Brown and watching the riders spin by. Soon I'm touching Malcolm's arm. "Did you see him?"

"Who?"

"Number 7. Watch as it comes round again."

Mal does see him when the car comes back round, and we both get ready to wave next time he goes by. Which we do frantically, but Hughie Jakes has no chance of seeing us. He's sitting all on his own and he's slipped into a tilt in one corner, making the car spin fast one way, pressing him into the back of the seat. He's hanging onto the safety bar for dear life, excited and scared, with his whole face scrunched up, loving it. I can't help feeling sorry for big Hughie, though. Single riders pay double.

Caught on Camera

Mam never was one to smile much, but I daresay she had a lot to put up with. It can't be easy looking after a large family at the best of times, and we could all be aggravating in our different ways, including Dad, whether he'd had a drink or not. She did her share of carping, but still got on with what everybody saw as her work in the house. There was one time, though, when she left Dad and that was all the fault of Fyffe Robertson and the BBC.

The first we hear that Ashington's going to be on the telly is when Vince comes round to fetch our Rose after he's been on the back shift. As soon as she claps eyes on him Rose asks, "What's that stupid grin for?" Vince is like an open book.

"You're looking at a TV star here, man," he says, doing a pose for us.

"What you on about?"

"The BBC's had its cameras up at the pithead. I got filmed coming out o' the cage and in the baths."

"In the baths?"

"Aye, from behind, like. Nowt rude on show. That's what the cameraman told us, anyway. We'll just have to wait and see, won't we?" He winks at me, fully enjoying himself.

"What's this for?" puts in Mam from behind the ironing. "There's not a strike brewing, I hope."

"Nothing o' the sort. You know the Tonight programme that comes on after the news? They're doing summat about how miners live now. Monday week it'll be shown. They're going to be all over Ashington filming for it. You might get yoursel' a part, Rose."

"They'll have to catch us first."

"Was Cliff Michelmore at the pit?" says Mam, interested because she never misses Tonight. Don't ask me why since it's the most boring programme on telly. I'd rather watch the Interlude.

"No, there was just blokes doing the filming. They're expecting Fyffe Robertson the morn, though."

"Which one's he?" from Rose.

"The one with the pointy beard," says Mam. "Ugly-looking feller. He interviews people on the street, that sort of thing."

"He'll have a job understanding half the folk round here," says our Rose.

"Well, they'll have the same bother with him. Whining Scotch accent he's got. Gets right on my nerves." And Mam attacks Dad's work pants as if she's running the iron over Fyffe Robertson.

Next day Malcolm, me and Derek Nesbitt go on the hunt for the TV people, with Nez scouting along the rows on his bike while we run to Station Road to see if they've parked themselves beside the shops. He catches us up by Doggarts.

"Just missed 'em at the top end," he yells, standing on his pedals. "We could've been in it an' all. They rounded up a load o' kids to make on they were playing footy in front of the pit heaps."

"Where they off now?"

"Feller with the beard was asking about Housey Housey. I think they're on the way to the Arcade." And he rides off in that direction, with us panting behind him.

Outside the Arcade there's a big green van with the words B.B.C. TELEVISION SERVICE painted in white and a cameraman in his shirtsleeves on its roof filming the front of the building. By the time we come running up Nez has already collared Fyffe Robertson who's with another bloke fixing a microphone to a long cable coming out the back of the van.

"Hey, mister, can we be in your programme?"

Fyffe Robertson straightens and looks down at Nez like he's sucking an acid drop. He's the first person I've ever seen wearing a bow tie in real life.

"Can we be in it? Me and me mates?" asks Nez again.

Fyffe Robertson contemplates us then points a thumb over his shoulder at a gaggle of women waiting on the pavement behind him. "Any of you boys belong to one of these fine ladies?"

"No, but we can make on we do," comes Nez, keen as mustard.

"This is News and Current Affairs, laddie, not BBC Drama. We don't do pretending."

Why rounding up kids to play football beside a spoil heap in the middle of the cricket season doesn't count as pretending we don't bother to ask. Instead we hang about while the crew sets up, in case we should be wanted to show off some other children's games. Conkers, maybe.

"Ready for level?" says Fyffe Robertson at last down the microphone and he starts asking the first wife her name and what she's had for breakfast, which seems to stump her so I'm hoping for her sake she doesn't get asked any hard questions. All the women have come out of the matinée at the Housey and Fyffe Robertson seems very interested in that, asking how many times a week this one goes and whether she generally wins or loses. Then he asks out of the blue, "And how much does your husband earn?" which proves another stumper.

"Eee, well, I don't rightly know," she says. "I mean I've never seen his payslip. I think it depends what shift he's in, 'cause say if he's in fore shift I'll generally get a tad more in the housekeeping..."

Fyffe interrupts. "That's the money he gives you to look after the home, is it? And is that enough, would you say, to care for your house and family?"

"Well, it depends what you mean by enough, doesn't it?" she says, looking a bit perplexed. "I mean, we could all do with more spending money but, you know, you've got to cut your cloth, as the saying goes..."

"And tell me, what does your husband do with the rest of his wages?" Fyffe comes back. He does have a queer Scottish way of talking like Mam says, all up and airy as if he's having a little joke with you. But underneath it seems to me he's being rude to this woman, poking his nose in, and kind of making fun of her without her really cottoning on.

He asks more or less the same questions to all the women and gets more or less the same sort of answers, though there's one or two get quite shirty with him and start pushing back when he pokes on about their men drinking and gambling.

"He's entitled to his bit pocket money," one woman says. "He works hard enough for it. Would you like to have to go down that black hole every day? I know I wouldn't."

They don't use this woman's interview in the programme, I notice, when it comes out the week on Monday. We've got a full house crowded round the box to watch it and we all cheer when we see Vince and his marrers spilling out of the cage near the start.

Our Rose gives a little squeal as she spots him lathering down in the pit baths.

"Vince Logan, I can practically see your backside," she goes, behind her hand.

Vince just laughs. "Shouldn't be looking."

Mal and me don't appear even in the distance but there's lots of blokes my dad knows, especially when they come to the part about the White House, the new social club at High Market.

"That's George Hall," says Dad. "He's the club secretary."

This bloke's quite proud of his new place and tells Fyffe Robertson it cost fifteen thousand to modernise. Fyffe Robertson calls it "luxury premises" and while we're watching men in the club drinking and playing dominoes he talks over the pictures claiming that the club is making five hundred and fifty a week from miners. My mam turns to Dad, goggling.

"Five hundred and fifty pound a week. How they raking that much in?"

"It's a big place," says Dad, his eyes fixed on the screen.

We see Fyffe Robertson sitting with some of the pitmen in the club and he's probing them just like he did with the women outside the Housey, trying to find out what they take home in wages. Most of them won't bite, but soon we see him with a couple of blokes, faceworkers younger than my dad, and one is quite happy to tell Fyffe Robertson he sometimes makes thirty quid a week. The other one says he has marrers earning up to forty five pound.

It's all gone quiet in our house, then suddenly there's an explosion from Mam. "Thirty pound? Forty five pound! A *week*!"

"They're having him on," goes my dad, twisting in his seat. "Look, you can see they're laughing and joking about it."

But when we look back at the screen it's filled by a close-up of a payslip with figures on. I can't make head nor tail of it myself, but somebody in the room can and she's raging.

"Here's me has to scrimp and save!" She stands up and wheels round to face my dad. "You *dare* tell me you're not earning that kind of money."

"Don't you raise your voice to me, woman. I've told you they've got it all wrong. That's probably an engineer's payslip, summat like that. Vince'll back us up."

"Leave me out of it," says Vince, looking a touch nervous himself by now and glancing across at Rose. "I'm not getting involved."

"Right then," says Mam and she points her finger at Dad like she does with us sometimes but never to him. "Let's see last week's payslip. If you're telling me that's not your wage, prove it."

"I don't have to prove it. I'm just telling you. And there's an end of it."

"I'll tell you the end of it, Frank, I'll tell you the end of it. If you don't get your arse off that chair and go and fetch me your slip from last week I'm going to pack a bag and walk out that front door and I won't be coming back. You've seen our Eddie do it, and you'll see me do it."

None of us moves in the room but it feels that we're all backing away except Dad who juts his chin out and taunts her like I've seen lads do in the school yard when they're squaring up for a fight. "Where you thinking of running off to, like? You've got nowhere to go. It's me puts a roof over your head. Nobody else. Don't you forget that."

"I've got places I can go, don't you kid yourself. Just you worry about finding that payslip. 'Cause you've got two minutes."

She stands there with her arms folded, watching him. The only sound in the room now is from the programme nobody's looking at any more. Dad moves forward out of his chair and I'm not sure whether it's to hit her or to go and do what he's bid. But it's just to turn the knob at the TV set. We watch the screen go grey except for the little white spot in the middle that's still fading as Dad picks his matches and Woodbines off the mantelpiece. He parks himself down again and slowly lights a fag, then sits smoking it in silence, watching the fireplace clock, defying her. After two minutes Mam walks out of the room and up the stairs.

Sure enough she packs a case and goes off, we don't know where. What we find out later is she catches the bus to Wooler where Mam asks Auntie Alice if she'll take her in. Meanwhile Dad makes Rose put a sick note in at her work so she can look after little Jeannie.

Mam is not the only one to have her feathers ruffled by the Tonight programme. It's caused such a row across town that it even makes the front page of the Ashington Advertiser. Whether other wives have upped sticks and left I couldn't tell you, but I know it's a miserable week.

That's how long the stand-off lasts between the two of them. Our Sally comes over a couple of times to help Rose but she has her own little one to look after. Mostly we have to shift for ourselves, Malcolm and me feeding mainly on cornflakes and Nestle's Milk sandwiches and Dad having to put his own bait up.

But nobody's tackling the hundreds of little things that Mam sees to every day and it doesn't take long for the house to get into such a state that even we can't help but notice. Jeannie's pining for Mam as well, sometimes working herself into such a paddy she won't be consoled by Rose or anybody else for hours.

On the Saturday morning Dad puts on the suit he wore for Sally's wedding, has Rose dress my kid sister in her little flowery frock, then hoists Jeannie up on his shoulders for the long trek to Ashington bus station. I stand watching them all the way to the top corner, shielding my eyes in the sunshine.

By the time they get back Malcolm and me have already given up on the cricket game we've been playing at the side of the house, since it's now too dark to see the ball. We're standing at our gate. My brother's doing keepy-ups off the bat, going for what he reckons is a world record 170 when he gets distracted, seeing them come along the street. Mam's in tow and Dad's cradling Jeannie who's fast asleep in his arms. Malcolm's ball slips off the edge of his bat and rolls towards them. Mam stoops and collects it, more like she's tidying up than fielding. She carries it until they get up to the gate and gives it to me, half-smiling. None of us exchanges a word, not wanting to disturb the bairn.

What Dad had to say for himself when he turned up on Auntie Alice's doorstep I have no idea but the following weekend Mam takes the three youngest of us to the Co-op where we all get fitted up with clothes for the new school term. A few days later a van rolls up to our gate with a brand new Hoovermatic twin tub washing machine. We get so excited about this that Malcolm and me stand in the scullery to watch it working for a week afterwards.

"Better than telly," claims Malcolm, and I have to agree. Better than the Tonight programme by a long chalk.

FALLING FORWARD

Tall in the Saddle

I'm the runt of the litter. Not that any of us amounts to much even full grown, hardly surprising with a mam coming in at well under five foot in her stockings, but I've always been the shortest of the short-arses among the lads.

I wonder if the jamb of the scullery door in our old house still shows the knife scratches where me and my brother measured up every now and again, the gaps between his marks always more than mine as he grew quicker. Me, I'm bigger sitting down than standing. I'm sure I owe my little legs to all them winter nights with my knees scrunched up against the cold, especially after a marble fight with Malcolm left a penker-size hole in our bedroom window. The council never turned up to fix it so it had to stay like that.

All of which explains the bother I have as a kid learning to ride on Alan Chisholm's bike. I can just about touch the pedals with my toes even after he's let his seat down. The only way I can move the bike is to perch on the crossbar, risking my balls as I wobble down the lane, with the saddle poking like a pistol into my back.

Alan's really good about letting me practise. He sits on the kerb reading my Wizard comic while I try and make it all the way round the block. If I haven't appeared by the time he's got to the end of a story he gallops round to find me 'cause chances are I've slipped sideways and got trapped under the frame or knocked the chain off.

Other times we'll ride down the dene, me sitting with my legs stuck out, hanging on tight to the edge of the saddle, leaning out the way of Alan's backside as he crouches over his handlebars, pumping up and down on the pedals. We always try to avoid the main roads when we're two on a bike. Not that we've got safety in mind, only there's less chance of bumping into his dad or one of the other coppers on the beat.

He's all right though, Mr Chisholm. PC Chisholm. I've liked him ever since Chiz and me first teamed up way back in the infants' when he took both of us along to the police station to show us the actual FA Cup. Jackie Milburn had brought it home to Ashington for some do at the Town Hall and he'd asked the police to look after it overnight.

I remember the shudder ripping through me as the key rattles in the lock, like I'm about to come face to face with a murderer, when Alan's dad opens the heavy cell door and ushers the two of us in. Instead of a cold killer there's the FA Cup sitting on a metal bunk that's screwed to the wall.

Alan's dad's voice booms around the hard cell, "What do you think of that, lads?" as proud as if he's won it himself.

"It's massive," we both say together.

"I'll show you how big it is," he says and with one scoop he lifts and dunks me into the top of the Cup. I'm nested there, gripping onto the sides, as if I'm on that lavvy I'm looking down at next to the bunk bed. Then he picks me out and does the same to Chiz who's squirming and giggling 'cause he's being tickled on the way. How many kids can say they've sat in the FA Cup? I wish we had a photo to show people.

Another reason I have for liking Alan's dad is that it's him I have to thank for my first bike when we're old enough to go to the junior school. He's clocked me trying out Alan's outside their house and caught us a couple of times riding two up, so when he gets the chance to find a home for an unclaimed bike he knows who to turn to. He takes us round the station yard to inspect it.

"I know it's not much to look at just now," he admits. "Somebody found it dumped in the bushes at Sheepwash and it's rusted up a bit, but nowt Brasso won't take off. You'll need some new brake blocks, mind, and don't forget to get yourself a lock."

The Brasso job takes most of the weekend and my finger is sore with rubbing in between all the spokes, but I'm quite chuffed with the result. There's a slow puncture in the back tyre so Alan shows me how to fix that and gives me some oil for the chain. When we go round to the bike shop I find I've only enough money for a lock or a set of brake blocks, not both.

"Hey, look, they've got them combination locks in," says Chiz, and that settles it for me. As long as I don't have to do an emergency stop, the brakes I've got will do until I can afford some new ones. Anyway I want to take my new bike to school on Monday so I'll need a lock if I'm not to get it nicked first day.

OK it's not a new bike and it hardly compares with Alan's Raleigh Lenton, but it's mine and I can reach the pedals from the saddle so as far as I'm concerned it's a treasure. And I love creating the secret of my new combination lock. I need a code I can easily remember but I reckon my date of birth's too obvious so I go for my mam's store number, 1626.

By Monday morning I've mastered the knack of braking long enough before junctions so that I slow down in time, but I've already had enough scares to realise I'm going to have to save up quickly for new brake blocks. Part of the trouble is I still can't properly reach the ground with my toes so the only way I can stop suddenly is to do a sort of scissor jump off my saddle and plant my feet on the road while I'm pulling the handlebars back, a bit like a cowboy with a runaway horse. I decide to call my bike Champion after the wild stallion on the telly.

There's no bike shed at the school, just an area back of the kitchens where you can park along the wall next to the bins. I thread the chain of my combination lock carefully through the front fork and spokes, shut my eyes to twist each number away from the secret code, then check I haven't accidentally put them back in the starting place. I repeat this three times before I'm happy with the numbers I've lined up.

As I'm cutting back through to the playground to meet up with Chiz I'm spotted by Colin Bone and Matty Cessford who must have come right over this way to do summat they shouldn't – smoke a dump they've found, maybe, or look at a mucky book. They're both in 3B so I generally don't see that much of them, which suits me if you want to know the truth of it. Boney calls out as I pass where they're leaning against the wall, "Hey boy, what you doing over here?" like he's massa and I'm his nigger. When I don't answer he shoves himself forward to block me off.

"I said, what you doing over here?" Cessford's taken up a position behind us.

"Nowt. Just parking my bike."

"Looking to nick one, you mean. You haven't got a bike."

"I have. Got it at the weekend. What's it to you, anyway?"

"Just interested. Aren't we, Cess? Howay, then. Show us your new bike."

They more or less push me back to where the bikes are parked and I have to point out Champion to them.

"Call that a bike?" scoffs Boney. "Where'd you get it, out the ark?"

"The river more like," comes Cessford, who's not far wrong as it happens.

"Look, he's frightened of getting it nicked," says Boney, inspecting the lock. "What's the combination?"

"Not telling you."

"Probably 1234. That's all he can count up to," says Cess, laughing at his own joke.

"Go on then, what is it?"

"Not saying."

Boney grabs my arm at the elbow and twists it behind my back. "What is it? Spit it out."

"1234!" I yell back at him.

"Don't get smart wi' me, boy. What is it really?"

Just then the whistle goes once in the distance. Then a second time and we see boys starting to run into their lines from their games in the yard. Colin Bone lets my arm go.

"Don't need to know anyway," he says. "I could have that off easy if I wanted. Piece o' piss. Only the bike's not worth the bother." He kicks the back tyre, then turns again on me. "Go on, get away you swotty midget," and in a sarky tone, "Teacher's waiting for you." He swings a kick at me while Cess bunches his fists up snarling, "Bastard teacher's bastard pet," as I run off to join the line going in to school.

All through morning lessons I'm worrying about my bike so when playtime comes I go rushing out to check on it, only to stop halfway when I spy Cessford and Bone leaning against that same wall at the far end. I trail back to the main yard where Alan is playing chucks with Dennis Freeman.

"You'll not get it pinched," says Chiz when I tell him what happened on the way in. "Not with your combination lock on."

Dennis Freeman snorts at this. "Combination lock? God, they're easy, them."

"What you mean, like?"

And Dennis gives us chapter and verse on how to open a combination lock. You have to keep the chain taut either end while you click through each wheel in turn, keeping your eye on the gap to the right of the number you're working on. When you happen on the number you're looking for the gap opens up a tiny bit and you can go on to the next number until you've got the whole combination lined up and the pin slides out.

I'm devastated. "That's knacked it, then. Colin Bone said it would be a piece o' piss and he was right."

"He's too thick to work it out," says Alan, still trying to keep my pecker up.

"Ah, he's got a criminal mind though, but," says Dennis, crushing it again. Dennis doesn't say how *he* got to know so much about breaking into combination locks.

For the rest of the day I'm half dying for school to finish and half dying at the thought of turning round the corner of the kitchens and finding my bike gone. At four o' clock the coast looks to be clear but Alan and me sneak quietly up to the parking place in case there's an ambush on the go.

Chiz can see over the tops of the big bins long before I can so he's first with the news. "Your bike's still there!" and we break into a run.

"Thieving twats!" is what bursts out when I get close enough to see. The bike's still there right enough, but my combination lock has gone.

"I could dob 'em in to my dad," Alan suggests as we're snaking slowly away from the school on our bikes. "He could prob'ly go round their houses and arrest them right now." I nod my head, but Chiz and I both know our lives wouldn't be worth living if we sent his dad in. You don't do that sort of thing in Ashington.

"Besides," I say out loud, "We haven't got proof, have we? You never know, it might have been somebody else." I'm remembering how I've been blamed before for things *I* haven't done. "Could've been Dennis Freeman pinching it for a joke, just to show he could. You know what he's like. Maybe I'll open my desk lid the morn and find he's put the lock there."

I'm even warming to the idea that this might really happen, playing it out in my mind, when I get a poke from Alan as we pass the gates of the swing park. We stop the bikes and look across at two lads clarting about on the teapot lid.

The one doing the spinning is Matty Cessford. Colin Bone is stretched out flat on top of the teapot lid, clinging on as it gathers speed. Cessford gets it going full tilt then leaps out of the way as Boney seems to slip off the top. We're expecting him to crash onto the ground but he doesn't. His body flies round with the teapot lid like he's an extension of it. He goes a few circuits before I see that he's hanging onto a chain that's looped around one of the bars.

He keeps up this Superman act till the teapot lid starts to slow down. First his body starts to twist around in the air then his legs buckle and his feet are kicking up dust as he tries to save himself from scraping along the bottom. Finally he lets himself go, rolling clear of the teapot lid, before chasing Matty Cessford across to the swings on the other side of the park.

I'm too far away to be sure but it doesn't take a genius to work out where Boney has got the chain he's locked onto the teapot lid. It's left dangling there while him and

Cessford entertain themselves chucking all the swings over the top of the frame, wrapping them round where no kids will be able to reach them. They're so intent on this that I make up my mind to rescue my combination lock while they're not looking.

I ride through the park gates keeping low over the handlebars as if that's going to make me invisible. I do a half-roll off the bike at the teapot lid and run to duck down behind it where I can't be seen from the swings. Softly I push at the bars until the one with the chain locked onto it comes round to me. All I have to do now is free the chain, get back on my bike and ride away.

Except I forget the combination. I'm staring at the numbers in a quiet panic and all I can bring to mind is 1234. After a long half minute I realise I'll have to give the Dennis Freeman method a go.

Hands shaking, I pull the chain taut either side of the lock. Trouble is now I can't stretch two fingers far enough to reach the cogs that change the numbers. I have to trap one end of the chain under my foot to free a hand. I start turning the first dial, watching the little gap to the right of it for any sign of movement as the numbers click through.

Sure enough when the dial turns to 1 the gap widens a fraction. I smile to myself, master safecracker, and maybe that relaxes me a bit because suddenly the whole combination pops into my head. 1626, Mam's store number.

I'm moving the second dial to 6 when I hear a sort of strangled Tarzan cry from behind. I turn to see Alan on his bike at the gate waving his right arm as if he's trying to haul me in. I lift my head slightly to look across the play area. Bone and Cessford are halfway between the swings and the teapot lid, running straight at me like a pair of guard dogs.

The alarm's gone off on the safecracker but I've come too far to give up now. I bend over the lock, giving the last two numbers my full attention. 2 and 6 fall into place and I draw out the pin then pull the chain away from the pole so hard it whips across my ear.

The teapot lid shudders. As I stand up I'm face to face with Colin Bone climbing over the deck towards me. He puts his hand out.

"Give us that here, you spakker."

Matty Cessford is coming round behind me, like he did in the school yard. I keep my eyes on Boney.

"It's my lock. You nicked it."

"Is it hell. I've had that for years. Giz it back."

"It's mine. It's got my secret combination."

"Some fucking secret," goes Cessford from behind and they both laugh, closing in.

Surrounded, I swing the chain over my head and they take a step back.

"Touch me with that an' I'll knack ya," yells Cessford.

I swing it in a bigger circle and they back off so far that Colin Bone trips over my bike lying on the ground. His mate looks across at him and I take my chance, pelting as hard as I can towards the park gates.

Even as I'm running I thinking, my bike, my bike. Alan's still on his, holding himself steady at the safety fence outside the park gates, urging me out. But he seems miles off.

Matty Cessford's running after me now, but I'm well ahead. Boney, though, has climbed onto my bike and he's getting up speed. As I get nearer the gates Chiz slips off his saddle and slaps it, a signal to me. He sets his right pedal to twelve o' clock ready for a quick getaway. I turn to check what's happening behind. Bone has passed Cessford and he's cutting the distance between us.

I face forward again, see Chiz waiting ... and suddenly I've got the widest grin on. I find an extra burst of pace just 'cause I know the faster I run the better this is going to be. I've seen into the future.

Chiz times his part superbly. He braces himself at the barrier to keep his bike steady as I do my leap, then pushes off as soon as my bum hits the saddle. The bike leans to one side then the other as he puts the effort in, then straightens out and we're away along Park Road.

There's a screeching and scraping from behind. I spin round in the seat just in time to see my bike, out of control, shooting out the gateway and smacking hard into the safety barrier. Colin Bone does an Olympic somersault, lifting off the saddle, pivoting at the hips and dropping right onto his arse in the road on the other side of the fence. He would have scored a perfect ten if it wasn't for the dodgy landing.

I've played back that move so many times in my head, it's become like a favourite film. Better than Tom and Jerry. Poor Alan missed it but I never tire of describing it to him or hugging myself inside when I think about the moment I saw it coming.

We come back to the park half an hour later to find the two thugs gone and my bike dumped over the wall with both tyres slashed. Still, it has survived the crash quite well, considering. Champion the wonder bike. Old-fashioned maybe but practically indestructible. Brakes a bit dodgy.

Chicken

"**R**ight, boys. Two to each cubicle. I want you changed and into the water in three minutes flat."

Everything's wrong about this. I lied to Dennis Freeman about being to the baths before. I got paired up with Porky Palmer on the walk over here and now he thinks we're best mates. I haven't a clue what we're supposed to do or where we're supposed to go. And I'm scared.

"Here's an empty one, look," says Palmer. "Let's go in here."

"There's not room for both of us."

"'Course there is. Leave the door open. Hurry up or we'll not be in the pool as long."

He keeps budging into me while I'm on one leg struggling with the double knots in my laces. Mr Thain is marching up and down the line of cubicles barking orders and generally winding everybody up. "Don't drop your things on the floor, laddie. Put them on the bench. Not in a heap like that. Neatly. Neatly."

"D'you think he'll let us in the deep end?" Porky prattles on. "D'you reckon? Hope he lets diving. I can go off the springboard, me. You know what my brother done? He dived right off the gallery. He did, honest. Right in the deep end. Like Tarzan, man. You know, a lad killed himself doing that once. Hit his head off the heater thing on the way down. You should've seen the blood in the water!"

"Did you see it?"

"Nah, but my brother's mate did. 'Course you get chucked out if they catch you diving off the gallery. But our Keith's done it loads o' times. You just have to wait till the woman's not looking. Dulcie she's called. He's gonna train us to do it after I've been off the top step o' the high dive. You know, the deep end's only five foot nine."

He peels off his shirt and shorts, throwing them into a heap on the bench then runs his thumbs under a silver chain he's wearing around his podgy neck. He turns to me, lifting up the disc that's strung onto the chain.

"See this? What d'ya think it is?"

I've no idea, but that doesn't stop me being jealous. It's a kind of medal with a picture made out of silver raised up so even if you were blind you could run your finger over it and feel all the details. It's some sort of Bible picture. There's an old man with Bible robes on and a long stick, wading over a river with a little boy on his back.

"It's a St Christopher," says Palmer. "It's dead old. Used to belong to my granda', then I got given it. You know the thing about the St Christopher?"

"What?"

"You can never drown when you've got one on. He's the patron saint of swimmers or summat. That's why I always wear it at the baths."

Mr Thain sticks his head round our cubicle.

"Come on, you two, hurry yourselves up. What are you still doing with your trousers on?"

"Just taking them off, sir."

"Get a move on, then. There's some in the water by now."

"I'm ready, sir," from Porky. "See you in there," to me, and he scampers off, his bare feet slapping along the stone floor as I slowly unhook my snake belt.

My bathing costume is a shock of red in the brown cubicle. There's a daft puffin badge stitched on that I've been picking at through my pocket on the walk from school but all I've managed to do is loosen the head so it flaps forward. Why didn't Mam get me a new one, a grown-up one? Why didn't Dad teach us to swim when I was little?

I poke my head out of the cubicle, listening for splashing noises to tell me which way to go. As I pad along the corridor a whistle blows and for a while all I can hear is my own faint feet, then Mr Thain's voice echoing as he shouts instructions to the class.

In a gap between the line of cubicles there's a trough of what seems to be grey milk that I have to plodge through on my way to the side of the pool where Mr Thain is standing in his tracksuit while the boys watch him from the water like seals. Their eyes all shift right as I appear through the gap and Mr Thain turns to see what they're all looking at.

"You're late, laddie. Where do you think you've been?"

"Toilet, sir."

"Speak up."

"Had to go to the toilet, sir."

"Should've done it in the pool," somebody says from below and a snigger goes round.

"Keep quiet down there." His eyes stay on me. "Well?"

"Sir?"

"What are you standing there for? Don't you think you've wasted enough time already? Get in the water."

"Yes, sir." I'm tiptoeing behind him when he clamps down on me. I can feel the hard metal of his wedding ring on my bare shoulder.

"Just a minute, just a minute. Where you off to now?"

"Into the water, sir."

"The water's down here, if you haven't noticed."

"Yes, sir, but the steps…"

"Steps?" he says, making on surprise like teachers do. "The steps are for getting *out* of the pool. To get *into* the pool…" He clicks his fingers and points at a boy in the water. "Clark, how did you get in?"

"Jumped, sir."

"Quite right. Palmer?"

"Dived in, sir. In the deep end."

"Right. Any of you boys take the steps? Anybody?"

Nobody speaks through the pause.

"So then," he says to me. "How are *you* going to get in?"

My stomach sinks into my bathing costume. "I… Can I go to the toilet, sir?"

"You've just been, laddie. What's the matter with you? Here, stand by the edge. Toes just over the side. Now, jump. It's easy enough. Come on."

I stand, looking past my toes at a dead cockroach floating in the white gutter. Water from the pool is slopping over the drain, gently rocking the beetle from side to side.

"Come on," I hear from far off as if somebody's trying to wake me up. Then closer, whispering in my ear. "Come on, you've got the whole class waiting. You can do it."

"I…"

"What?"

"I can't, sir."

"What do you mean, you can't?"

"I don't know how. I've never…"

"Right." Mr Thain peeps sharp on his whistle. "Everybody out."

"Howay, sir, we've only been in five minutes," moans Palmer.

"You're not finished yet. I want everybody along this edge here. Line up. Straight line. That's it. You..." He shuffles me sideways like he's shifting furniture. "You join on the end like so. Good."

He paces behind the line of boys at the pool side. There's a draught at my back from the opening into the changing rooms and I'm shivering.

"Now, listen. We're going to show this boy how to jump. Not yet..." he warns as one or two teeter on the edge. "Don't move. Don't move a muscle yet. When I touch you, then you jump. Not before. Ready. Go! Go! Go!"

On each "Go!" a boy flies over the edge and splashes into the pool. I'm watching a line of people getting shot in the back one after another. It's coming to me. I turn from the line and look up. I need Batman to swing down from the roof and save me. There's that heater the lad hit his head on. There's the gallery. There's a splash right next to me. Who is it? I can see 4ft 6in on the white tiles in front. I'm too little. There's a shove into my back. I'm falling. It's too deep. I'm in the water. Over my head. I can't feel the bottom. Where's the bottom? I'm drowning, I'm drowning. Something there. Grab onto it. Grab onto it. And there's a great rush of water as a dolphin pulls me up and out to the precious air.

"Get off, man. Get off, you're chokin' us."

It's not a dolphin. It's Porky Palmer. And I'm hanging on for dear life to his St Christopher.

"Leave off," he yells again. "You've got me strangled here."

"Oh, you've saved us, you've saved us. I was drowning, man."

"You'll fall in," I warn him.

"Got it," he grunts, and he plays the rope through his hands as he creeps backwards to the main branch. "Here, you grab on when I swing it across and you can have first go."

"I'm not chancing it. Did you not hear that branch creakin'? Somebody'll end up in the river."

"Get away, it's been here years, this tree. Safe as a house. You're just too scared to go on. You're chicken."

"Don't call me chicken."

"Chicken." He stands up on the branch, holding onto the rope and starts squawking, flapping his arms. "Waah-wa-wa. Chicken. Waah-wa-wa."

"I'm not a chicken, you fat pig," I shout back.

"You, chicken. Me, Tarzan." He gives out a loud Tarzan cry, leans back slightly, then dives off the branch with the rope between his hands. At the bottom of his swing the rope shudders. The branch dips and the rope starts spinning instead of swinging, turning Porky round and round over the river. He looks across to the bank with a frightened face, then we both look up at the branch, knowing it's going to break any second now.

But it doesn't. The rope turns slower and slower until it's almost stopped and the branch stays dipped with all Palmer's weight under it, but it doesn't break. Porky's about ten feet away from the bank and he looks at me so mournfully I have to laugh. Talk about Tarzan. He looks more like Pussy in the Well.

"Help us," he mews.

"Get stuffed. You're just gonna have to get wet. I'm away home."

"You canna leave us, man. D'you know how deep this river is?"

"It's only a short swim. Chuck your shoes and socks onto the bank first."

"I can't swim that far. Not in deep water."

I can't get my head round this. "You said you could swim in the baths."

"Well I can, sort of. But I have to keep one foot on the bottom a bit. I've never really been in the deep end."

"Ah, you stupid, lying... What did you swing on the rope for?"

"To be Tarzan. I thought it would come back to the bank so I could jump off."

"Can you not climb up to the tree?"

"It's a hard enough job hanging on here. Me arms is killing, man. You've gotta help us, quick. I'm gonna fall in."

I look at the river under Porky's feet. It does look dark and deep. The end of the Tarza is dangling just a couple of inches above the water.

"Hang on, I'll be back in a minute," I tell Palmer and I dash away from the bank leaving him yelling after me 'cause he thinks I've done a runner. It takes me longer than I promised and Porky's desperate by the time I come back with a dead branch I've found in the woods.

"Look," I says to him. "I'll save you, but you've gotta give us summat, right?"

"You're not having me St Christopher."

I hadn't thought of asking for that and for a second I wish I had, then I tell him what I really had in mind.

"You've to give me them two birds' eggs you've got, OK? Deal?"

"Deal. Howay, man, I'll drop if you don't get a move on."

"Listen. Slide down as far as you can. Right to the end of the rope."

Porky lets himself cautiously down the rope. The tree seems to dip dangerously again, so I run to the edge of the bank and hold my loose branch out as far as I can towards him.

"Here, grab onto this. Go on, stretch out. Get a good grip."

He grabs and misses a couple of times, and that seems to help because it makes the rope sway just enough to let him hold on to the branch the third time he tries. I haul him in close enough for one big pull to land him like a monster catch onto the bank. He drops onto his knees with a "Made it!," taking all the glory for himself.

"Hope you haven't smashed them eggs," I say and he feels in his pocket, bringing the pair out intact. I put a hand out for my prize.

"Bugger off," he says, but he hands them over quick enough when he sees me pick that dead branch off the ground. I put the eggs in my pocket next to the pair he gave me earlier.

"Frigging thief," he spits out as he gets up to go. I stay where I am on the bank, watching him into the woods. He disappears, then comes back a few steps to yell at me. "Anyway, if you think I'm gonna be your mate after this you've got another think coming. And you can stick those eggs up your arse for all I care." With that he gives me a V sign and retreats into the woods.

I wait at the bank until I'm sure he's well away then I slip into the woods by the track we used earlier to come down to the river. It takes me ages to find the spot, but at last I'm back at the bottom of the tree with the snapped off top.

Slowly, much more slowly than Porky Palmer climbed, I make my way up the trunk, then into the branches to the broken part. Not daring to look down, I stretch to the place where he stretched until my fingers can feel the cup of an empty nest. I try to keep that place in my mind's eye while I bring my hand down to my pocket and slowly up again. As carefully as I can I place the four eggs back in the nest.

I stay there for a minute, cooling my face against the cold of the tree, then inch my way down, using my feet to seek out safe branches and knotholes. It's already dark by the time I'm back on firm ground peering through bushes to find the path that leads out of the woods to home.

A Merry Dance

We're not used to girls in our playground. Once infant school was finished with they stayed behind the green fence while we marched through into a whole different country called Junior Boys.

Standing at the border I can see and hear the differences. Our side is mainly barbarian, bossed by Chinese burns and half nelsons. There's a few quiet huddles swapping cigarette cards or singeing the backs of hands with a magnifying glass, but the most comfortable-looking kids are the ones wrestling on the ground, crushing into corners or mounting the cuddy with Superman dives onto other lads' backs. Even the football game at the bottom of the yard is a cheerful mass battle with up to sixty kids chasing the ball at any one time.

Our side is a mad din of whoops, yells and machine gun noises. What I hear from the other side is chants and chatter. The chants come from the bobbing heads around the skipping games, the pairs practising two-bally against the wall or in the air, and the player hopping through her turn at baysie. The chatter is from the dozens and dozens of girls gathered in their twos and threes around the yard who all seem to have exciting news or secrets to tell each other.

I can see guards with white tea mugs patrolling both territories but on one side the lasses are forever fluttering in and around them like moths while on our side blocks of lads move away from the patrol like it's an icebreaker coming through. The men teachers never talk to the women over the border line. It's as if the two countries have separate languages along with all their other different ways of going on.

But there is one time every summer when the gate in the green fence is opened and a year-group of girls comes filing quietly into our yard where their teachers make them stand in a neat row facing boys of their age who have been made to wait shiftily for the last ten minutes in a more or less tidy row ready to meet them. This year I'm in that line.

It's two weeks before the 59th Annual Ashington Children's Gala, a fortnight before every kid in every junior school in town sets off to join a parade ending at the gates of the Hirst Welfare where they'll be handed a shiny new half crown before passing through for a day of sports, games ... and country dancing.

From the window of our classroom there's a long flex that stretches all the way to a piano stool parked near where the two tribes stand avoiding each other's glances. Balanced on top of the stool is a gramophone that looks as if it's been made by a carpenter to last a hundred years. Underneath is a small pile of 78s.

A woman teacher with butterfly glasses steps forward.

"Boys and girls, I know you have been told about our big day coming up and I'm sure you're excited about it. We are all together this afternoon to start practising the dances that we are going to perform at the Gala. It's really important, isn't it, that we get everything right for your mams and dads and all the hundreds of people who are going to be watching on the day. So boys, the first thing I'd like you to do is to pick out a girl of around your height and bring her to the space behind me."

There's movement from some of the lads but it's away from, not towards, the queue of girls. A few even make on to be climbing the wall behind them to get away. Others are shaking their heads violently or pretend-praying to be let out of here. Meanwhile the lasses are giggling and whispering to each other as they look sideways across at our line, weighing us up I suppose.

One girl has her big eyes on me as her friend whispers something urgent in her ear. To be honest the reason I notice is I've been watching her since the teacher asked us to choose somebody our own size. Judith May was in the same infant class as me. She's still a dot compared to some in the group but she's easy to pick out with the white ribbon in her dark brown pony tail and her summer frock that little bit more showy with no cardi on top.

"Well, what a shy bunch we have here, girls," says the woman in glasses. "And some silly ones too. Should we show them how to be sensible and grown up?"

There's a few nods and "Yes, Miss Stephens" from the girls, though most look as unwilling as our lot. "Well then," she carries on. "Let's try it the modern way. Ladies, I'd like *you* to pick a partner and bring him to the space behind me, please."

My heart bumps with shock when a flyer from a friendly push in the back brings Judith May tumbling gawkily across, a wide grin on her pretty face. My own face is scarlet when she tugs me away from the line of boys who whistle and call out as she makes us the first couple to stand behind Miss Stephens. Other bold lasses follow her lead, then a few more, but it's left to both groups of teachers to start coaxing and threatening until we're all paired off in one way or another.

Miss Stephens organises us in sets of four pairs each and sooner than you'd think we're stepping and twirling through the Eightsome Reel, the Gay Gordons and the Dashing White Sergeant while Jimmy Shand and his Band wheeze out of the school gramophone.

Before the end of this first practice I've fallen in love with Judith May. I'm in love with how she claps her hands lightly in time to the music, in love with the smile and little nod she gives me whenever the teacher calls out "To your partners", in love with the touch of her waist on my arm and the breath of air she leaves as she spins away, in love with her energy and the fun we're having secretly together among all this counting and circling and crossing and back.

Standing in the middle of the usual commotion of the yard next day I can hardly believe this is the place the dancing happened or that Dennis Freeman, who's hollering at me from the top of the yard, was just yesterday on the opposite side of my circle hand in hand with two girls, skipping sideways.

"Can't hear what you're saying," I shout back at him as I'm running up.

"I said you're wanted at the fence."

"Who by?"

Without answering he tugs me in that direction. Marilyn Wright, Judith's friend, is on the other side of the fence, peering over into our yard. As we come up to her I notice Judith in the distance, her back against the girls' building, one foot resting on the wall, one hand pulling on a wisp of hair, her face turned away. Marilyn Wright looks round as if she's checking for spies, then pokes a piece of paper through the railings at me. It's a note written in pencil on lined paper:

You can go with me if you want. Tell your ansr to Marilyn. J. xx

I quickly fold the note up and shove it in my pocket, then tig Dennis so we'll have an excuse for scarpering. He tigs me straight back and runs off. I make to chase him but turn towards the fence for a second and shout across at Marilyn, "Tell her yes," before I go sprinting after Dennis.

Nothing happens and I don't see Judith again until the next dancing practice. She's exactly the same as the first time except that when Miss Stephens stops the music to give us some instructions Judith doesn't let go of my hand. I put our hands behind my back to hide them from the others.

On the Thursday after tea I'm riding around back of our block looking for the ice cream van when who should I see sitting on a rug in the sunshine at a gable end but Judith May and her friend Marilyn. Judith waves at me so I bump over the kerb and cross to where they're cutting paper dresses out for a little cardboard figure that's propped up on a stand between them.

"Do you live round here?" I ask Judith.

"In the flats. She's number 5 and I'm 7a."

"You should know where your girlfriend lives," Marilyn chips in, and they both giggle at each other.

Judith pats the space beside her which I take as a command so I park my bike and sit on the rug with my back against the wall, watching them play with the different paper outfits they've cut out, hooking them onto the shoulders of this flat doll. Nobody says anything for a bit, then Judith picks up a paper party frock in each hand and holds them up to me.

"Which one's nicest, d'you think?"

"Dunno."

"I'll try them both on her." First she hooks the blue flouncy one on the doll, then the bright yellow one. "Now which one?"

To me she looks best in the neat pink and white petticoat she wears underneath but I say the yellow one.

"D'you think?" she says doubtfully. "Which would suit *me* best?"

"Er, the blue one?"

"It's lovely, isn't it." She plucks at her own skirt so it sticks out like the flouncy dress and crosses one foot over the other, pointing her toes like a ballerina. Then she leans back, stretching her brown legs along the rug.

I hear the chimes of the ice cream van coming along the road. I sneak my hand into my shorts pocket and finger the threepenny bit there, wondering what to do next.

Marilyn gets up off the rug. "I'm away to ask me mam for some money," she announces. Judith watches her disappear round the corner then turns quickly and kisses me so suddenly on the mouth that my head hits the brick wall and my eyes prick. She keeps her lips pressed against mine for a few seconds, and I can feel one of my bottom teeth moving, then she draws away, looks me full in the face, and lightly licks the tip of my nose.

I've still got my hot hand on the threepenny piece in my pocket. I take the coin out and show it to Judith. "Would you like an ice cream?" I say.

The day of the Gala we have to line up in the boys' playground two by two with our dance partners as if we're going into the ark. I'm as scrubbed and tidy as I ever get and Judith is the bonniest lass in the yard in her polka dot dress, white ankle socks and new sandshoes. As we parade out of the school gates Miss Stephens is shouting up and down the line, "Hold on to your partner's hand. Everybody must hold hands." Judith's had mine in hers for the last quarter of an hour.

We stream along the middle of the road with grown-ups and toddlers watching us from pavements. At some corners we have to stop to let another school join the flow.

"There's the Holy Rollers!" one lad shouts and a chant starts up, "You Catholic bugs, lift up your lugs..." till Mr Thain hauls somebody out of the line for a strapping and nips it in the bud.

We have to go the long way past the Central Hall. By this time we've even got a brass band heading the parade and I'm swinging Judith's arm to the beat as we turn into Alexandra Road. Then we come up against a tailback as kids queue for their half dollars at the gates of the Welfare. At last we arrive at the row of tough-looking men in flat caps dishing bright silver out of cloth bags, like they've just robbed the rich to give to the poor. It feels weird to be taking a coin at the entrance instead of handing one over to get in.

Kids, teachers, parents and bandsmen are swarming all over the sports ground yet somehow the man with the megaphone gets everybody organised for stagecoach races, egg-in-spoon races and what the man calls "foot running", which as far as I can tell is the same as ordinary running. Our Malcolm is second in his age group for that and wins a certificate. Me and Alan Chisholm are down for the three-legged race but we're not well-matched for size and he has to drag me along like a limp until I fall over and we get disqualified.

I'm not so clumsy when I switch partners. The country dancing is the highlight of the day, with the whole of the main field taken up with sets from every school and the outside railings crowded with parents jostling for a good view. Judith takes charge of our group, arranging us in a circle and getting us to hold hands and smile at each other while we wait for the first piece. In the moment before the music starts she stands perfectly poised, just the edge of her dress fluttering slightly in the breeze. I can't see where my mam is but I can guess she's looking at Judith and saying, "That lass has been here before," meaning life not the dancing.

All three pieces go perfectly as far as our set is concerned. Tell you the truth, I've no idea about the other groups 'cause I only have eyes for Judith. It's as though the sun is her spotlight. She leads me everywhere with the faintest touch of her fingers or just drawing me in with a glance, and she somehow makes us the centre of every pattern in the group. Everyone's attracted by her.

Afterwards she drags me across to find her mam at the other side of the railings. Her mam reminds me of the woman from the cover of the Littlewoods catalogue with no coat on and a white purse in her hand that she opens up to give me and her little girl sixpence each.

Judith takes us both off to see her Safety First poster at the Arts and Crafts Exhibition where she meets up with Marilyn and the two of them walk round the displays as if they're joined at the hip, leaving her mam and me to trail behind them. I get my eye on the outside door after a while so I take a step in that direction, saying, "Thanks for the sixpence, Mrs May."

"You deserved it, pet. Danced like angels, both of you," she says. "You'll have to come over for tea sometime, eh?"

That night I'm lying awake, too hot, pushing my tongue against my wobbly bottom tooth, wondering when I'll get to see Judith again. Not much chance at school with the Gala finished. But I know where she lives now and I know her mam so maybe I could just go and seek her.

Easier said. I bike round the flats next day and there's a bloke outside cleaning the windows so I'd have to go past him to get to the door. Plus I can't remember whether it's Judith at number 5 and Marilyn at 7a or the other way on. Not wanting to go knocking at the wrong flat I ride home instead.

Next day I try again. Nobody's around the doors outside the flats, but as I turn at the corner of the block I spot Judith playing on her own at the gable end. She's got no shoes or socks on and her skirt's tucked into her knickers while she's bouncing a ball through the back of her legs onto the wall and catching it with her other hand, singing some rhyme to herself.

I sit on my saddle at the kerb behind her watching her practise until she misses a catch and turns to chase the ball rolling away. She sees me and grins.

"Caught you looking," she says, pulling her skirt free but in no hurry about it. She picks up the ball and lobs it at me. "Try and hit us," she says and zig-zags away in her bare feet.

I let the bike down with a clatter and chase after her with the ball. As she slips round the corner I let fly and she whoops when the ball misses her and bounces against an outhouse in front of the flats. By the time I've followed she's disappeared, just the ball lying at the bottom of a drainpipe, but as I'm bending down to pick it up the outhouse door opens and it's Judith going "Ssh," and beckoning me in.

Inside is a big washing machine, a sink and a bench. This must be some kind of washhouse for the people in the flats to share. Judith shuts the door behind us and stands with her back to it.

"Caught you looking, didn't I?" she says.

"What?"

"Want to see?" She reaches down to the hem of her skirt, then stops and smirks at me watching. "Only if you show me yours, mind."

I say nowt but I'm still watching as she lifts her skirt up with one hand and pulls the front of her navy blue knickers down with the other. We both stare solemnly at her pink triangle, then she lets the elastic snap back and drops her hem.

"You now," she says.

I don't know how I should do it. In the end I just feel under my pants and pull it out of a leg of my shorts, holding the cloth up as if I'm going for a pee.

Suddenly Judith's whole body shudders as someone rattles the door. I get such a fright I piss a drop or two and I have to clutch myself to stop and soak it into my underpants. Judith jumps clear of the door as a huge woman in a pinny comes in with a wash basket.

"Mind out," says the woman.

"Sorry, just getting a drink o' water," Judith chirps, squeezing past her and through the gap with me in tow covering my damp patch.

"Who's that laddie? He's not from round here," the woman says as I sprint off.

I cock my leg over my bike at the kerb and wheel it round to face home. I look across to check whether Judith's watching me go, and see Marilyn Wright coming out the doorway of number 5. Judith grabs her excitedly and pulls herself up to Marilyn's ear. I know what she's saying because Marilyn claps her hand to her mouth and both girls nearly end themselves laughing as they watch me ride off up the road.

Sometime through the night my loose tooth finally comes away and in the morning I wake up with it sticking to the outside of my cheek. I take it downstairs, where Mam and our Rose are having tea and toast in the kitchen.

"My tooth's come out, Mam. Can I put it under my pillow to get sixpence?"

"No fear," says Mam. "You're too old for that mullarkey."

"Ah, Mam," says Rose, teasing. "Fancy shattering his illusions. You still believe in fairies, don't you, sweetheart?"

"No."

Rose reaches out as if she's going to caress my face. I can feel a fleck of her nail varnish in the corner of my mouth as she presses the bottom lip down and inspects the gap in my teeth. "Ooh," she goes. "Who's been kissing the girls?"

And I blush to the roots of my hair.

Digging

Me and my brother Malcolm were maybe the only kids in Ashington who never looked forward to the Miners' Fortnight. Not to the first week anyway. While our friends went off to Butlins or Blackpool, or at the very least on day trips to Whitley Bay or Saltwell Park, the two of us were left facing the big dig.

Having the largest back garden in the estate was heaven in November when there was bonfires to be built but hell under the July sun when Dad stripped down to the waist and led us through the jungle, bound for slavery. All year the garden was a wilderness until that week when our job was to turn it over completely and cart the weeds away before we had any hope of visits to the seaside.

It didn't stop us dreaming of freedom though. Malcolm struck the right note one afternoon when he got us started on negro spirituals.

"John Brown's body lies a-mouldering in the grave; John Brown's body lies a-mouldering in the grave..."

Even Dad joins in. "John Brown's body lies a-mouldering in the grave, but his truth goes marching on."

Then we're all in on the chorus. "Glory glory Halleluiah. Glory glory Halleluiah. Glory glory Halleluiah. His truth goes marching on."

"Wouldn't be surprised if we find a body somewhere in this lot," grunts Mal, hacking at the long grass with his spade.

We don't come across any corpses, though we do find a couple of old tennis balls, a few burnt-out fireworks and a rusty cap pistol buried among the weeds. Uncovering an odd treasure like this is about the only thing that relieves the monotony, apart from playing chicken with the traffic as we trundle our bogey across the main road to dump another load into the ditch next to the railway line.

Malcolm points out an excursion coach as we're waiting at the kerbside. "See that? It's on its way to Scarborough." We've never been to Scarborough but we know there must be a beach there. The name went right through a stick of pink rock that Auntie Florrie fetched back for us to break our teeth on last summer. As the coach rolls by we stand with our barrow watching the passengers observing us curiously through the windows as if we were natives of a strange land and they hadn't just got on at Ashington bus station.

Back at the digging, the sun starts to tell on our neck and shoulders and sweat streams down Dad's sides as he toils away with the garden fork. It can't be much of a holiday for him either, just working in a different direction attacking stones and clay same as he does with rock and coal underneath the ground.

At bedtime we can't bear the sheets on our sunburn. Anyway it's too hot to lie underneath them. Every night's a struggle between discomfort and dog tiredness with sleep just about winning out in the early hours, not long before the light comes streaming through the curtains again.

The one saving grace about having Dad as a taskmaster is the job gets finished on time. In fact we're nearly a day ahead. We generally pack in around six o' clock but on Thursday we keep on going with the end in sight. By quarter to eight Dad's leaning on his spade at the top of the garden while Mal's giving me a lift across the soil in the empty bogey.

"You know, Dad," he says, "If we flattened this out and put turf down we could play football an' cricket an' all sorts on here. It's big enough."

"Aye, maybe we'll do that this year," Dad half-agrees. "I'll have a think on it. Good job, boys. Really good job." He even has a treat planned. He's got Mam to buy a bottle of cream soda off the pop van and he manages to catch Robbie's Ices on his late round so we can have ice cream floaties in it. Best summer drink bar none. Plus from his own pocket Dad gives me and Malcolm two bob each to spend for the good job we've done.

Even though we've finished a day early there's no chance of Dad agreeing to fit an extra day trip in – Morpeth and Whitley Bay have to wait until next week – so Malcolm and me decide we'll use our earnings to go to the beach at Newbiggin on our own. Or nearly on our own. Paul Hutchinson is kicking round our door on Friday morning so he decides to tag along.

"Tell you what," says Malcolm. "'Stead o' using the bus let's get the train to Newbiggin."

"I shit in Newbiggin train," comes Hutch, sniggering.

"What?"

"That's what it sounds like, dunnit? Ashington-Newbiggin train. I shit in Newbiggin train."

My brother just looks at him like he does with me sometimes. "Grow up," he says, dryly. He's eleven.

On our way to the station we climb up to poke our faces over the side of the railway bridge and catch the steam off a coal train coming through. We'll be riding on one of the new diesels, cleaner and faster, but you can't beat the smell of the old steam engines.

Malcolm takes charge of all the money and ticket buying. Mam's told him he's responsible for bringing me back in one piece so when we're coming in to Newbiggin station and I pull the compartment window down to watch for the platform he yanks me in again. "There's people had their heads knocked off doing that," he yells. I can't help glancing back down the line as we get out at the station even though I'm not seriously expecting to see any severed heads lying on the embankment.

We spend some of our money even before we get out of the station. On the platform there's a machine that lets you print your name onto a strip of aluminium, threepence for up to ten letters. The alphabet is set out round a dial with a pointer in the middle. You have to turn a pointer round to face the letter you need, then press a lever to stamp the letter onto the strip.

Malcolm goes first then he puts another threepence in for me to have a go. I'm really careful, slowly turning the pointer and checking before I stamp and move on to the next letter.

"Howay," moans Hutch. "The tide'll be in before we get to the sands at this rate."

"I'm making sure I get it right. Nearly finished." But as I'm checking the dial to find the next letter Paul Hutchinson leans across the lever, stamping a v where a v shouldn't be.

"Oops, sorry," he says, not meaning sorry.

"What you do that for?" demands Malcolm while I'm looking down at the ruined strip, tears starting.

"It was an accident," claims Hutch.

"Was it hell." He pushes Hutchinson up against the station wall. "Give him thruppence for another go."

"I haven't got thruppence."

Malcolm clips him and Hutch charges back, practically pushing them both off the platform onto the track. I look over my shoulder, anxious about trains, but what I see is the bloke from the ticket office steaming up to us.

"You boys trying to kill yoursel's?" He bundles them both away from the edge of the platform and up the sandy steps. "Hadaway afore I get the police in."

I follow them to the top of the steps where Malcom says, "This way, youngun," and reaches past Hutch to draw me in then starts walking me quickly along in the direction of the prom with his hand on my shoulder. Hutch falls in behind until Malcolm stops and shoves him back. "Piss off. You're not coming with us." And he steers me away while Paul Hutchinson stands with his hands in his pockets watching us go.

I suppose it's doing the garden together that's made us so close. Malcolm acts as a tour guide pointing out all the delights of Newbiggin-by-the-Sea. He takes us the long way round to the prom past Bertorelli's where the penny arcade is. There's loads of folk gathered around, some licking ice creams, some perched on the quay wall looking across to the lifeboat station and Church Point.

"We'll play the slot machines on the way back, eh?" says Malcolm. "There's the shuggy boats, look. Should we have a ride before we go in the sea?"

He dips into our kitty and soon we're heaving on ropes to make the boat swing. When my end goes down all I can see is my brother looming up like he's going to topple into me any second, laughing. As the swing tips up I catch a picture of the sea with people plodging all along the shoreline, a few deeper in to swim, the pleasure boat out in the waves and a glimpse of Blyth in the far distance.

Later we park ourselves in the sands below the middle shelter so we'll have a landmark to find our clothes when we come back from swimming. Lots of people have the same idea so it's pretty crowded round that part of the beach and we end up well away from the prom. As soon as we're stripped down to our cossers we pick our way through the camps of people, then run as fast as we can across the flatter sand to dive into the waves.

Or at least Malcolm dives. I wade in up to the point where the waves hit the bottom of my trunks then come to a halt, clutching myself. "It's freezing!"

"Dive right under, man," calls Malcolm, twenty feet further away. "It doesn't feel cold once you're in properly."

Just then a bigger wave rears up and knocks me backwards. The water rushes over my head and I feel the sand sucking at me as I struggle to right myself, panicking. Another wave knocks me shallower and I can poke my head out of the water where Malcolm's on the lookout.

"There y'are," he says. "It's better when you're all the way in, eh?"

We mess about in the sea till our hands go crinkly, then we run along the edge of the sand to the rocks. Lots of grown ups as well as kids are there collecting wiliks but we've got nothing to save them in so we spend our time looking in rock pools for crabs and starfish, picking up slimy seaweed to burst the bubbles as we go.

At the bottom of one of the pools Mal spots a threeppenny bit and picks it out.

"Maybe someone threw it in there for luck," I suggest.

"Well, it's lucky for me now," then seeing my face he says, "Tell you what. When we get back to the railway station you can put it in that machine so you can print your name out properly."

"OK. Thanks."

"Bags you carry it, though," he says. "I've got no pockets in these trunks." And he hands over the coin for me to hang onto while we do some more exploring.

Before long it turns cooler and we're getting sprayed with sea water as it crashes over the rocks. "Tide's coming in," says Malcolm. "We'd better make a move."

Plenty have thought the same and there's very few folk left on the sands at the middle shelter.

"Where's our things?" says Malcolm, looking about.

"They were just here ... somewhere." But the little pile of shirts, shorts and shoes we made seems to have disappeared. Apart from some half buried shells and a crumpled biscuit packet one family has left behind all we can see on this section of beach is sand.

"This *is* the middle shelter, isn't it?" I look up at the prom to check, and find myself staring at Paul Hutchinson standing on the bottom bar of the rail with his elbows crooked over the top bar, watching us. We clamber across the sand towards him.

"Lost summat, have ya?" he says over the bar.

"What have you done with our stuff?" says Malcolm, still mad with him.

"I've been looking for yous for ages. It's boring on your own. Where you been all this time?"

"Where's our stuff?" demands Mal again.

"Oh, was them clothes yours down there?" Hutch comes back all innocent. "I thought somebody must've left 'em behind. I buried them."

"Buried them? What the hell for?"

"Dunno. Summat to do."

"Well, you can bloody well dig 'em up again," shouts Malcolm.

"You're the boys for digging, aren't ya? Why don't *you* do it? They're your clothes."

"You wanna get back home tonight?"

"Yeah."

"You'd better come down here, then. Where d'you think all the train tickets is? And the rest of the money."

Hutch slips down from the prom onto the sands and starts surveying the scene.

"What you waiting for?" says Malcolm.

"I'm just getting me bearings."

"Did you not put a marker down or summat?"

"I buried them behind the windbreak."

"What windbreak?"

"The green one. Well, it's been taken away now like," says Hutch, then quickly to stop Malcolm hitting him, "But I know where it was. Across here, look. Start digging here, we'll find them no bother."

The three of us start scrabbling around in the area Hutch has pointed out but we find nowt in the sand except a few pebbles and some dried up seaweed. Behind us the tide has already covered the flat part of the beach and is spreading itself our way.

Malcolm starts directing matters urgently. "Make a wider circle. You dig around this side. Hutch, here. I'll try nearer the prom." We go at it like dogs searching for a bone, throwing the sand backwards between our legs and every so often shuffling sideways to attack a new patch. I'm a bit hampered as I'm still carrying the coin Malcolm found in the rock pool so I park it between my lips while I'm digging.

Just as my skinny arms are flagging I feel something soft under my fingers. I burrow down and grab with one hand, then take the lucky coin out of my mouth to yell "Malcolm!" as I'm pulling up. It's one of my own black sandshoes. Water fills the hole I've made as if the shoe has been acting as a stopper, then more water flows around me and I realise the tide has caught up with us.

The other two run quickly down to my part of the beach and we all dig furiously while the sea water seeps around us. I find my other sandshoe straight away. A minute later Hutch comes across Malcolm's short-sleeved shirt covered in wet sand. Then the water rises higher and we have to give up, splashing back to the steps and onto the dry promenade.

"Here's your shirt, anyway," says Hutch, holding it out. Malcolm snatches it as he moves towards him like my dad when he's got the belt in his fist. "See ya!" from Hutch and he sprints away from us along the prom. My brother starts giving chase but he treads on a pebble with his bare foot and has to pull up, cursing. Talk about hopping mad.

I catch up with Mal and put my shoes on while he's examining his sole. The sun's weaker and I'm shivering, feeling exposed in just my trunks now we're away from the beach. My brother's even worse off – at least I've got summat to protect my feet. "What'll we do, Mal? How we gonna get home?"

"We'll have to walk it," says Malcolm.

"Walk it?"

"It's only three or four miles. I've done it before."

"Not with just your cosser and no shoes on you haven't." I open my hand with the coin in it. "How much is the train fare?"

"Fourpence each."

"Oh."

Malcolm clicks his fingers. "Hey, lucky coin though, but. It helped you find your sandshoes,didn't it? Why don't we try it in the slot machines? We could maybe win enough money for the fare."

"Oh, right. Suppose." I'm looking a bit forlorn at this point, tell you the truth. Not that this usually works on Malcolm. But he's definitely got a dose of brotherly love this holiday.

"Sorry, I promised you could have it for your name printing," he says.

"'S alright. Anyway *you* found it. We might as well have a go at the slotties."

"No, a promise is a promise. Howay, we pass the station on the road home. You know what, we could cut across the fields once we get out o' Newbiggin. That'll be easier on the feet, plus we'll prob'ly get home quicker."

Malcolm throws his soaking wet shirt over his bare shoulder and leads the way to the railway station like a Boy's Own hero while I shuffle behind respectfully, feeling guilty about having shoes to wear and being about to spend all our money on myself.

At the station there's quite a crowd waiting for the next train, some with rugs or windbreaks under their arms, kids hanging onto buckets and spades, bags bursting with towels, one or two beach balls, a bloke carrying a tin pail that must have at least a hundred wiliks inside along with a few lost creatures crawling over the top of the pile trying to feel their way back to the rock pools. Luckily there's no queue at the printing machine so I dash across to feed my coin in and block out all distractions for the next three minutes as I print the letters slowly onto the metal strip.

We're climbing out of the station to start our long walk home when who should we see skipping down the other side but Paul Hutchinson, halfway through an Orange Maid. He's just about to bite another chunk off the lolly as Malcolm dips under the centre rail then up with his shoulder into Hutch's chest, sending ice skidding over the steps. Malcolm wrestles Hutch down and starts feeling through his pockets.

"What have you nicked?"

"Nowt. Get off, will ya?"

He grabs at Malcolm's wrist and they struggle, ripping his pocket as Malcolm snatches his hand away and half turns, still pinning Hutch down on the steps, to show me what's he pulled out. Three rail tickets snipped at the corners. He turns back to Hutchinson, digging his knee in. "You bastard."

"I wasn't nickin' 'em."

"Liar."

"Just keeping 'em safe when I buried your pants. It was just a joke. I was gonna say but you went mental so I thought, stuff 'im."

"I'll frigging well stuff you."

The steps shudder slightly and I hear a noise from the platform below. "Train's coming in, Malcolm," I say, anxious about missing it and about the two of them starting another fight. Mal stands up, still looking down at Hutch, and presses a bare foot in the middle of his chest.

"You were gonna let us walk all the way, so see how *you* like it," he says. With that he takes one of the three tickets, rips it into shreds and sprinkles the pieces over Paul Hutchinson. "Howay, kidder," he says to me and we race down the steps to join the queue for the train.

Naturally enough Mam goes spare when we arrive at the house half an hour later with barely a stitch on. Malcolm gets the brunt of it since she'd made him responsible, but he never once dobs in Paul Hutchinson. He makes up some story about our clothes getting washed away off the rocks but she's in no mood to listen to the details. The only thing that saves us from the belt is the work we've done in the back garden, which is just as well 'cause I was wincing at the thought of the strap on top of my sunburn. All next week's day trips are off though and Malcolm's in a right bad fettle when we're sent up to bed.

"It's just not fair," he moans. "After we've slaved on all week. We'd be better off at school."

"Might as well be," I agree.

"I can see why our Eddie buggered off as soon as he got the chance. I'm gonna do the same. Soon as I'm old enough I'm joining the navy. I'll be outta here like a shot."

Which saddens me since in spite of everything I've had one of my best days ever with Malcolm. One of the best weeks, even. Usually I'd be clapping my hands to hear him talk about leaving home, but it's been different these holidays.

I reach down under the bed and take out something I've been keeping in my shoe. "Here," I say to my brother, giving him it. "I made this 'cause of you losing yours in the sand."

There's still plenty of light coming through the bedroom window so he can see that the aluminium strip I've given him has the name Malcolm stamped on it. To be quite honest it doesn't exactly cheer him up, and he hasn't a word to say about what I've done, but before he lies back on his side of the bed he slips the shiny name plate carefully under his pillow. So I guess in his own way he's glad to have it.

Head Down

Sally did. Eddie didn't. Rose did. Malcolm didn't. I'm next in the sequence, then Jeannie of course, though it'll be a few years before she has to worry about her eleven–plus. According to the family pattern I'm due to pass and further down the line Jeannie will fail. Unless you look at the order in a different way. Girl passes. Boy fails. Girl passes. Boy fails. So then I fail and Jeannie passes. By the time my little sister has to think about exams the pattern will be clear and she'll know what to expect. Right now I haven't a clue.

At home I'm supposed to be the brainy one but I reckon that's just because I'm more likely to pick up a book than Malcolm is. And what does that prove? I've only ever seen Rose read women's magazines and she got into grammar school, even if she did leave before her O Levels so she could work at Culpitts and start saving for her bottom drawer. Anyway, do Just William and According to Jennings count as proper books? Is that what they read at the grammar school? I wish I knew.

One afternoon I've got my head down in The Coral Island and I hear Mam saying to Auntie Florrie, "He's in a world of his own when he's reading them books." I'm not sure whether she's pleased or complaining but anyway she can't be right, can she, not if I can hear her saying it. I blush and put my head down further, feeling like a fake.

At school I don't know where I stand as I keep having to change where I sit. In 4A it's all about how close you are to the window and how far away from the teacher. When

I start in Mr Neville's class he puts me on the dark side of the room about halfway between him and the back wall which is about where Malcolm ended up so Neville has me down as the same stamp. With his system, though, people are moved up, down and across every Friday after the dinner break.

When you get the call you have to scoop all your belongings out of the desk you're in and move lock stock and barrel to your new place, while the boy who was there is on the move as well. Sometimes it's a straight swap but more often than not there's lads dodging up and down all the aisles with arms full of exercise books and pencil cases. God help us if we bump into each other and send our stuff flying 'cause that not only brings Neville's strap out, it puts us another couple of places down the pecking order.

The only boys who never have to leave their desks are Austin Cooke and Nigel Forster at the back desk by the window and Willie Mordue, the kid with the glass eye who Mr Neville always keeps right by him at the front. As they'll be the first to tell you, Cooke and Forster are the brains of the class, constantly vying with each other to be top in the mental arithmetic tests. Nobody really knows how Willie Mordue ended up in 4A. Probably the teachers reckoned it would be too dangerous for him to be with some of the lads in the other classes. As it is he's forever losing his glass eye in the playground. He'll peek sheepishly around the classroom door with one hand clapped under his specs and Mr Neville has to send the lot of us back into the yard to look for his missing eyeball.

How the teacher works out his ranking system I'm not altogether sure, but I don't think it's particularly scientific. It seems to be some vague combination of marks in tests, how often you've had the belt that week, whether you're tidily turned out and what mood he happens to be in on the day he decides. He must find it difficult to weigh me up. I've been to just about every point on the compass by the end of the first term and I'm still moved on a regular basis halfway through the year though he's gradually settling me into one or other of the middle rows.

Apart from moving desks what 4A is all about is tests. Twice a week the room is electric as Mr Neville paces up and down the aisles, stopping every few seconds to fire a sum at one of us from close range then grabbing a wrist for a swift, single execution with the strap if we take too long to stammer out an answer or have the audacity to get it wrong.

Otherwise tests mean practice papers for the eleven–plus that we have to plough through while the teacher sits at the front marking the last ones, his radar always switched on for the slightest noise. I work close to the paper, wrapping one arm over in a sort of cocoon, with the smell of the varnish from my desk part of the dull peace until Neville decides I must be up to no good buried down like this and sneaks along the aisle to rap me over the head with his knuckles.

One morning in March we're given a test paper first thing. It's not the normal start to the day and summat else that makes it odd is Mr Carrick turns up and watches us for a while as we work. Plus Neville spends more time than usual walking up and down the aisles saying nowt and not even cracking heads.

We're no sooner finished the arithmetic paper and coming up for air when he dishes out an English test and we have to go under again. Then he hands us one of those tests I quite like with puzzles and answers you have to choose from a list, some of them a bit like ones I've seen in the Boy's Own Annual. We're still busy with this when the bell rings for playtime and we bob up expecting to be let out, but Neville growls, "Carry on what you're doing." We work on as more and more lads tumble through the corridor into the yard, yelling and calling, and we're still working when the whistle's blown and everything's gone quiet again.

At last, just when I'm bursting for a pee, Mr Neville calls a halt. The monitors collect in the papers and he tells us we can have five minutes' play outside. 4B must have been told the same thing a shade earlier as by the time we emerge there's already groups of them hanging about or strolling around in twos and threes like prisoners in an exercise yard.

"You know, I think we've just sat the eleven–plus," ventures Alan Chisholm.

"Get away, we would've been told. It'll only be another practice. Bound to be."

But it turns out Chiz is right. Mr Carrick comes swooping in from his office again to confirm it and to tell us the results will be with the school sometime in June. "And I'll say this to you boys," he says in that W C Fields way of talking he puts on when he's making a speech, "With such a fine teacher as you have in Mr Neville, it wouldn't surprise me to see a substantial pass rate from this class. In fact I expect it and you can go home and tell your parents I expect it."

Of course I don't tell them any such thing. I never mention what goes on in school or pretty much anywhere else for that matter. What I do instead is go home and worry.

My stress level rises when I check in my Collins Gem dictionary and find that I should have chosen *eccentric* as the word closest in the list to *idiosyncratic*, not *idiotic*, climbs higher when I tip my marbles onto the bed and prove that 18 is 75% of 24 not 27, and hits boiling point when I sit up in the middle of the night with the horrible realisation that HAIR is to HEAD as BEARD is to CHIN not MOUSTACHE.

I'm beginning to grasp that I'll soon be following my brother to the secondary modern. He's happier there since he won his place in the football team but one of the things that concerns me is the number of lessons he seems to have on metalwork and carpentry, not to mention the ones on shifting chairs in the dining room and picking litter off the school field. Also I'm pretty sure that Chiz'll be away to the grammar school and maybe even Dennis Freeman so who am I going to be left with? Willie Mordue?

Same as we weren't told about the day we had to sit the eleven-plus, so we have no idea that we're about to get our results, until one Thursday morning in June when Mr Carrick breezes in. Our bums have hardly touched the seats after morning prayers and we have to jump to attention. He loves all that respect and he stands with his chest puffed out for quite a while before his hand lifts to waft us down again.

"Boys," he says grandly, "I'm proud of my school. I'm proud of this class. As is your teacher Mr Neville." Our teacher Mr Neville stands next to him demonstrating his new-found enthusiasm for his class by nodding like Bengo. He'd wag his tail if he had one. Mr Carrick goes on.

"I have here the results of this year's eleven–plus examination." He holds up the folder he's carrying as proof, like that gormless Prime Minister did when he came back from seeing Hitler. "Only three boys in the whole of 4A have failed the test. Only three."

Which three? My pulse is throbbing. Which three? Willie Mordue, obviously, but who are the other two? Me and who else?

"Your individual results are on these pink slips which you must take to your parents for signature. I'm going to place them face down on your desks and you are *not* to look at them until I give the command. Arms crossed, face the front."

We sit paralysed but our eyes follow as Mr Carrick importantly riffles through his folder, and pads each slip down with his fat fingers, first on Willie's desk then the rest of Row A, Row B, Row C where I'm sitting this week, Row D... 36 places, 3 failed, that's what ...12 to 1. 18 to 1 if you take Willie out of the running. Good odds you'd say, but all the worse if you're one of the losers. I look down at the pink slip on my desk. Usually the paper we get handed out is so cheap you can read what's on the other side. This thicker stuff must be from County Hall.

"You can turn them over now."

I do nothing for a few seconds, too weak to move. At last I manage to gulp some air into my lungs and reach out, then hesitate, caught by the sight of Grant Stevens in Row B. He's further forward than me and I can just see the right side of his face and his head down towards the paper that's turned print side up on his desk. Grant Stevens is crying. From now on every person in this class will remember Grant Stevens as the lad that cried when he found out he'd failed his eleven–plus.

Who else? Around the room boys are looking at each other smiling, clapping their partners on the back, miming like Harpo Marx as they daren't shout out loud with the teachers watching. Even Willie Mordue is beaming round at the others. He's not bothered to look at his result. And Grant Stevens is crying in the middle of it all. Nobody else upset as far as I can see.

So Willie is one, Grant is two. I flick over my pink slip. My name written in black ink over a dotted line. The same thick nib has scored out one of the words PASS/

FAIL in capital letters below, leaving the other one clear to read. Sally did. Eddie didn't. Rose did. Malcolm didn't. David did.

For the first time ever I bike across home at lunchtime to tell my mam the news. She's pleased, but not as chuffed as I hoped she'd be even though I know she's not one to get excited. I suppose she expected it more than I did and I guess part of her is thinking about the cost, what with a new uniform to pay for since there won't be owt of Malcolm's to hand down. One good thing is I won't have to take the bus to Bedlington, like Sally and Rose did, now there's the new Ashington Grammar next to People's Park. I decide to ride past it on my way back to school, and I find Chiz has had the same idea.

"Looks all right, eh?"

"Big though, innit? We won't have a clue which doors to go in."

But at least we know we'll be facing this together, and we're pretty cheerful as we're pedalling side by side, talking over how things are going to be. It's only after we get parked up back at school that the trouble starts.

"There's another two!" some kid shouts as we're walking through the yard. I don't twig this means us until a knot of lads from 4B suddenly turns into a lynch mob and chases after me and Alan. We're grabbed and pinned back by the arms. I'm already wincing, waiting for a smack in the face, but the gang gets organised and we're frogmarched at full speed to the bottom of the playground with a guard either side of me and a second pair behind with Chiz.

The space between the toilet block and the outside wall makes a sort of alcove that we generally use for a goal at the bottom of the yard. Today it's been turned into some kind of holding cell. There's more than half of 4B lined up to stop people escaping and as the line opens to let our guards shove us through I can see that the eight or so lads already trapped inside are all from 4A.

I bump up against Paul Miller. "What's going on?"

"Dunno. They keep pulling people out an' they don't come back."

"Bloody hell. It's like the Jews."

Next thing Paul Miller and Maurice Pitt both get dragged out and marched away. A minute later I'm watching Nigel Forster's petrified look as he's yanked through to God-knows-where when Colin Bone pokes his head past the bodyguards to check who's left. His face lights up when he sees me. "I'll have this little bastard," he says and squeezes into the cell. I make to kick him but before I can connect I'm charged down by the nearest yob in the line. Him and Boney have me trussed up in no time, and I'm half-dragged, half-carried in the same direction as Nigel Forster, which is towards the toilet block.

Needless to say Matty Cessford is in on the act, standing with his leg jammed across the entrance to the lavs. He lets it down when he sees his mate coming and gives me a yellow grin as I'm bundled through, saying, "Have a nice time, scholarship boy."

I can hear Nigel Forster wailing in one of the bogs as I'm hauled past the piss trough and bumped through the far lavvy door. He's going, "Get off! I'll tell on you, I'll tell!"

A voice says, "You breathe a word an' you'll get this every day till the end o' term."

"You an' all," Colin Bone hisses in my ear as he grabs the back of my neck and forces me onto my knees in front of the lavatory pan. He holds me right over the dirty bowl and the smell is sickening. There's a muffled moan and the yanking of a lavvy chain next door.

Through watery eyes I can see Nigel Forster's matching red pen and propeller pencil come rolling through the gap under the dividing wall as the toilet flushes. Now it's my turn. Boney stetches across to pull the chain over my head then leans all his weight to press me down into the bowl. All I can do is scrunch my face, holding my breath as the water comes swirling in, drenching my hair and splashing up to my eyes, nose and mouth.

There's a deep gurgle from the bog as the water sucks away. I have to open my mouth for air but as I do the smell hits me again and I retch into the bowl. The spew is still dripping from my mouth as Colin Bone yanks me up by the collar.

"Aggh, filthy, fucking pig," he says and pushes me away from him. I slip down between the bog wall and the lavatory pan where claggy pieces of Izal toilet paper are sticking to the damp floor. Colin Bone looks down on me in disgust. "Not so fucking smart now are ya, grammar school boy?" Then he hauls me out of the mess and shoves me in front of him out to the yard like he's carrying a piece of shit on the end of a stick.

As we're passing Cessford at the door another pair of 4B lads are rushing up to the toilet block with Grant Stevens in their clutches. Stupidly I find myself starting to say, "But he *failed* his..." Grant Stevens gives me such a look of stony hatred I'm stopped in mid-sentence and he's hurried off into the bogs. Colin Bone plants a foot flat on my arse and catapults me away from the scene. "Blab and you're dead!" he yells as I make my way through groups of kids playing out their own war games, wiping my face and my damp hair with both sleeves.

"Maybe it happens every year," Alan Chisholm is saying as we bike home together after school. "Like a tradition."

"I've never heard of it."

"You should ask your Malcolm."

"He would have said."

I shut up for a bit after that, thinking about Malcolm and what side he'd be on, and remembering the look Grant Stevens gave me as they pushed him into the toilets. Chiz breaks into my thoughts.

"We'll be rid of them after the summer, anyway," he says. "All the friggin' morons. Pack 'em off where they belong."

It's my feeling guilty that makes me snap at him. "Are you calling my brother a moron?"

"What you on about? I never mentioned your brother."

"You did, good as. Just 'cause he's not at the grammar school, doesn't make *you* the better person."

"I never said I was. What's got into you, like?"

"Nowt. I'm just saying ... You wanna watch what you're calling folk, that's all I'm saying."

I don't realise for a minute that Chiz has jammed his brakes on until I turn for another gripe at him and find he's not there. I look round and spot him way off, perched on his saddle at the kerbside. I make a U-turn and pedal back to where he's parked.

"What's up?"

"If you gonna be like that you can ride on your own."

"Howay, Chiz. Let's not fall out about it. Not after the day we've just had. You're still me best friend, man."

Chiz looks down past his crossbar and for the next couple of minutes he says nowt, just sits on his saddle, kicking away at the pedal that's nearest to the road. The sun streams over my shoulder, catching the silver bits of the pedal as it turns. Both of us watch the pedal spinning round and round as if we're being hypnotised.

Chiz finally snaps out of it, looking up and past me at the school building beyond the park before he speaks. "I never said your Malcolm was a moron."

"I know you didn't."

"He's OK. I like him. He's funny. Funny ha-ha, I mean, not funny peculiar."

"Aye, he's all right." He's got me smiling to myself at the thought of my brother. And I'm thinking, rough as he is sometimes Mal wouldn't force anybody's head down a toilet. Bet nobody would stick his down one neither. I reach across to tap Alan on the shoulder. "Tell you what, I wish I'd had our Malcolm with us in school today. He would've knacked the twats." I wait till I see Chiz grinning, then I follow up with, "Howay, I'll beat you to the park gates."

Naturally Chiz wins easy with his racer, which suits me 'cause all I'm wanting to do is cheer him up. By the time we split off to go our different ways home we're best mates again. I watch him riding up the park path on one side of the new school and wait till he disappears before I wheel my bike around to ride along the road where the main gate is.

By this time the grammar school's finished for the day as well, so I find myself passing older lads and lasses walking home, some on their own and some in company, all wearing the same navy blue uniform and mostly carrying big haversacks, homework I suppose. Others, lads mainly, are riding bikes same as me along Green Lane, heading home for their tea. It will only be a few weeks before I'm joining them for real. I can't imagine how different it's all going to be.

Behind The Stories

As I mentioned in my introduction I thought readers might find it interesting to read press accounts of some of the real–life incidents that find their way into these stories. I am grateful to the News Post Leader for permission to transcribe articles from the *Ashington and District Advertiser* and *Ashington Advertiser* and to The Journal for allowing me to reproduce extracts from their coverage in *The Newcastle Journal* of the Munich air crash.

First up, however, is a line drawing of the Woodhorn Colliery disaster memorial featured in *Old Man Tate*. I placed it accurately in my story in what we used to call the 'flower park' area of Hirst Park, between the side gate and the paddling pool, where it was erected in 1923. It stayed there until 1991 when it was moved at the request of Bob Howard, son of one of the victims, to Woodhorn Colliery Museum. The statue and plaques are still as I describe them in the story. The original miner's lamp was missing for many years, perhaps the result of vandalism by children raking the streets and public places of Ashington. The statue was provided with a replacement lamp when it was relocated to Woodhorn.

The first of the newspaper snippets, dated 20 September 1957, is a report of an inquest into the deaths that occurred as a result of the real–life event, a van falling into the River Wansbeck, referred to in *Steady*. Some of the people involved in this unfortunate accident were friends of my older sisters but the story I have weaved around it is fictional. For narrative purposes I moved the location and the day the crash happened from a Friday to a Saturday, but otherwise the account Rose gives of the accident coincides with the facts. The newspaper article is fascinating not least for the unsensational coverage of the bravery displayed by the constables who came to the rescue and for the casual attitude shown at the time not only by the young men at the centre of the incident but by the authorities to the issue of drinking and driving.

The next press cutting, dated 20 December 1957, is one of several light-hearted pieces in the newspaper around that period covering the 'new' craze of Housey Housey, which is central to my story *Light Fingers*. The pastime quickly grew from once a week to every day for some, including matinées. A colourful fairground operator by the name of Jack Richardson was the entrepreneur behind the Arcade Bingo – in fact he was literally behind it as he lived in a very swanky caravan round the back. When I was a lad it was my job to deliver his newspaper, which meant I had to run the gauntlet every day of his voracious Alsatian guard dog, Major. There's food for another story, yet to be written.

Next comes the local coverage of the Munich air crash in February 1958, the pivotal event recounted in *Babes*. There is so much I could have included here, not only of the accident but of the dramatic football matches immediately before, the unexpected recovery of Matt Busby tempered by the death two weeks after the crash of the promising Duncan Edwards, the renaissance of Manchester United, and the silver lining emergence of Bobby Charlton as a star England international. For the purposes of illustration, however, I have selected part of the news of the accident as it was carried in the North East regional newspaper, *The Newcastle Journal*, including a local interest piece about Bobby Charlton from the same issue. To provide an insight into one of the central characters of my story I have also added a feature on Cissie Charlton (or Elizabeth to give her Sunday name) that was published in the *Ashington Advertiser* on 18 April, 1958 when her son Bobby was first selected for the full England team.

From July 1958 I have included one of two front page reports from successive issues of the *Ashington Advertiser* about the way BBC Television's *Tonight* depicted life in Ashington, which is the subject of *Caught on Camera*. The article neatly summarises the local furore created by the programme and provides an interesting commentary on social and family attitudes of the time, as well as reminding us what inflation has done to the value of our money in the intervening years.

I have included the *Ashington Advertiser* account of the 59th Annual Ashington Children's Gala, the event that forms the centrepiece of my story *A Merry Dance*. Incidentally, although he does not appear in my tale, it is interesting to see the name of Will Owen MP mentioned in this article. *Advertiser* editors of the time were always highly respectful of their local Member of Parliament, that is until the 1970s when he was branded a Soviet spy and proven to have enjoyed two decades in the pay of the Czech intelligence service.

The real-life incident that sparked my leek show story *Washed with Milk* is reported in the *Ashington and District Advertiser* for 30 September 1960. In my version the victim of the leek-slashing incident is portrayed as Josh, a character loosely based on my Uncle Jabez, a champion grower. In real life the unfortunate gardener happened to be the father of my best friend from school. I have also included a column on leek show uses and abuses from the same issue that comments on the people who, like Frank in the story, cheerfully enter shows and win prizes without having gone to the trouble of growing the leeks themselves.

Finally I have reproduced an *Advertiser* report about the strange rumour that swept our part of Northumberland and inspired my tale of *The Black Monk*. It actually happened in October 1964 and I remember it very well as a pupil at the time of Ashington Grammar School. The school ran along one side of People's Park, the supposed home of the monk in our version of the rumour. For narrative purposes I have shifted the date to coincide with my earlier time in the junior school but the delicious terror we felt en masse is I hope faithfully recalled.

David Williams

Woodhorn Colliery Disaster Memorial

From the Ashington & District Advertiser Friday 20 September 1957

Young driver tells about death plunge

It was revealed at Monday's inquest on two young men who lost their lives when a motor van crashed through a fence and plunged into the River Wansbeck that one of them – James Edward Douglas (23), of Bywell Road, Ashington – died of heart failure when trapped in the submerged vehicle.

The other victim – Harry Jolley (23), of Tenth Row, Ashington – was drowned, and his body found under a shelf of rock in the river the following day.

William Rickard of Newbiggin Road, driver of the van, and George Lawrence Coutts, of Simonside Terrace, Newbiggin escaped by climbing on to the vehicle as it lay in the river. They were rescued by Constables Joseph Kelly and John Leslie, who were commended by Coroner Hugh Percy for a "brave effort under such difficult conditions."

Coutts, in evidence, said the party of four arrived in Morpeth at about 8.15 on the Friday night of August 23, and visited three public houses. At the first each had two glasses of cider and two bottles of stout, at the second two half pints of beer, at the third a half pint of beer, a glass of cider, and a bottle of stout.

* * * *

Weak Heart

Dr. J.B. Davison said that both bodies had traces of alcohol in them when a post mortem examination was carried out. Concerning Douglas, the doctor said:

"He had a diseased heart and any shock or severe physical exertion could have killed him at any time."
"He probably had the disease for some time previously and was unaware of it."

Coroner's Comments

Coroner Percy said in his summing up: "There is no suggestion that the driver was under the influence of drink in the sense that he was drunk."

"At the same time it seems to me rather sad to think that youths of this age should, in one and a half hours or thereabouts, have consumed this quantity of drink in three public houses."

"Of course the laws of this country – although I think personally, unhappily – do not prescribe that cars must not be driven after the consumption of alcohol. How far that exact co-ordination between mind, hand and foot, which is so essential for safe driving, may be impaired by alcohol we do not know," said the Coroner.

"We must not assume because an accident has occurred that it was due to alcohol," he added.

* * * *

Through Fence

A statement made by Rickard on August 24 was read by Sgt. J. Byers. In this he said that he left home about 7.25 p.m. on August 23 to meet Coutts at a Laburnum Terrace, Ashington, cycle shop. "Then" he continued: "Harry Jolly and Jimmy Douglas came along."

They went to Morpeth, drank in three public houses and then had a supper of chips, peas and egg, at about 10 p.m.

He was driving back to Ashington, with the roads wet, and had just arrived at the series of bends near East Mill when he felt a sensation of skidding. He put on the foot brake but they went through the fence into the Wansbeck.

He got out on to the side of the van.

"I have never had such an amount of drink before when I have driven a van but I was certainly not drunk," he had said.

Mr. Hedley Proctor, of Hawthorne Cottage, Morpeth, said that he was driving towards Morpeth from Ashington when he saw pieces of wood in the roadway. He stopped to clear them away, and then noticed the van in the river.

It was a very black and showery night: the sort of night when he did not like driving, he said.

* * * *

To the Rescue

P.C. Kelly found a number of cars parked near the scene of the accident, one of them shining its lights upon the van, which was on its side, 15 feet from the bank. He immediately stripped, and with a rope swam out to it. The river was not in spate but there was heavy rain.

After taking the survivors off the submerged van P.C. Kelly tried to get the body of Douglas out. P.C. Leslie went to his aid. They took the ignition key from the dashboard and opened the rear door to recover the body.

There were 35 feet of railings broken down where the van entered the river, said P.C. Leslie. On the other side of the fence was eight feet of bank and an eight feet drop to the river. The van was five or six yards out into the river.

* * * *

The Verdict

Mr. Percy said there was very little evidence to go on to satisfy the jury as to the cause of the accident. The driver said he felt a skid and there was a possibility that the van had skidded.

The jury returned the following verdict:

That the deaths occurred in accordance with medical evidence by reason of the car leaving the road, the reason for which is not clear in the evidence.

They added a rider stressing the urgency for this part of the road to be made safer.

From the Ashington & District Advertiser Friday 20 December 1957

IT'S JUST A KID'S GAME
BUT IT'S FUN

The craze that has them all in a daze	Fell-em-Doon reporting	Here the women's tongues are still

For the men it's great news. A way has been found of keeping women quiet and at the same time happy. This 20th Century miracle has been achieved by housey-housey, the latest craze in Ashington and other pit villages.

To see large crowds of women happily silent you have to visit a large scale housey get-together like the one that does business once a week at the Arcade, the largest public concert hall in the town.

There each Wednesday night from 7.30 to 10, if you are a member, you can join about 400 other people – mostly women – who concentrate passionately on a simple kid's game, once the pastime of bored and browned-off soldiers and sailors.

Here, because there is money in it for a lucky few, your can see 400 people reverently bent over their numbered cards and covering figures with tokens as the numbers are drawn at random from a bag and shouted by callers at the silent fascinated players.

Fifteen numbers must you cover on your card to win a prize of £2 or £3, and the quiet breathless tension mounts as the cancelled out numbers begin to pile up.

* * * *

A Winner

Suddenly someone somewhere in the packed hall exultantly cries "full house". Most probably it is a woman, for the women far outnumber the men at these astonishing affairs.

The tension snaps. Tight shut lips open, still tongues begin to wag. The beehive comes to life, buzzing noisily. The surging tide of talk is a mixture of congratulation, relief, envy and large dollops of disappointment. Everybody tells her neighbour how near she was to hitting the jackpot...if only...if only...

Briskly the completed card is publicly and loudly checked, then the caller sings out "house correct", and they need no appeals or exhortations to shut up. They are eager to get on with the next round. No preacher in Ashington ever received such absorbed attention for prayer or sermon as do these business like dialect speaking callers as they declaim numbers, and still more numbers, nothing but numbers. Like a blanket silence falls again on the great gathering. To miss a number would be disastrous.

Some drag deeply at cigarettes as they crouch over their cards, some suck sweets while others abstractedly munch potato crisps all handily available at a snack bar counter.

* * * *

Counter Styles

And housey housey is not without its fashions. There are intriguing preferences in counters which the players use in covering up the numbers.

Some use neat, plastic ones, others utilise tiddley-winks, some cover-up with shirt buttons, and at least one favours white back studs, which, being fitted with a tiny knob, are easily picked and put down like tiny ivory chessmen.

One woman player candidly admits that she genuinely enjoys Housey-Housey every night in the week. All insist they are having fun, and certainly between sessions the animated, friendly groups round the tables appear gay and free of troubles.

* * * *

The Thrill

It is, of course, the money they're after, and from my own experience of having a go with one half-a-crown card, it can be darned exciting waiting for only two numbers to come out of the bag for a completed card and a "snowball" or cumulative prize of £10.

On the other hand a good time is being had by all. No effort is needed, and we are all Geordie's bairns together.

*   *   *   *

Thought for Others

In the background is the intention to use profits for the purchase of a large television set for the local hospital so that a handful of winners, the large army of losers, and the hard working organisers of this kid's game with grown-up money prizes may feel that what they are doing with their nights and spare cash is not entirely a wasteful, self-interested enterprise.

From The Newcastle Journal Friday 7 February 1958

SOCCER PLANE: 21 DIE
Seven are Manchester United players

CRASH AFTER
TAKE-OFF

SEVEN OF MANCHESTER UNITED'S SOCCER STARS DIED YESTERDAY WHEN THEIR PLANE CRASHED AFTER TAKING OFF FROM RIEM AIRFIELD, MUNICH.

Altogether 21 people, including some of Britain's top sporting journalists, perished in the disaster.

There are 23 survivors, but many of them are seriously injured.

CAPTAIN AMONG DEAD
Heading the list of dead was United's captain and English international left-back Roger Byrne.

Others killed were Mark Jones (centre-half), Bill Whelan (Eire international and inside-right), Tom Curry (United's trainer and former Newcastle and Stockport County player), Eddie Colman (right-half), Bert Whalley (the club coach), Tommy Taylor (United and England centre-forward), David Pegg (outside-left and an English international), Geoff Bent (left-back), and Walter Crickman (club secretary since 1926).

Frank Swift, the former England goalkeeper turned journalist, died in hospital after an operation. He had a fractured skull.

LOCAL SURVIVORS

Team manager Matt Busby, also in hospital, was said by doctors to have little chance of survival.

Among the survivors were Ashington-born Bobby Charlton, inside-right, and Ray Wood, reserve goalkeeper, who comes from Hebburn.

Another who escaped was Margaret Bellis, 37-year-old stewardess, from Darlington, and formerly of Whitley Bay.

The plane – a specially chartered B.E.A. Elizabethan – was bringing the players home after Wednesday's drawn game against Jugoslavia's Red Star in Belgrade.

It had landed at Munich to refuel.

THIRD ATTEMPT

Players and journalists were joking in the airport waiting-room while the air liner was refuelled before its final "hop" to Manchester.

Snow was falling as the plane taxied out at 2.45 p.m. It returned.

Twenty minutes later it went out again. There was another delay.

Then, at the third attempt to take off, onlookers heard its engines rev-up, saw it start forward.

ENGINE CAUGHT FIRE

Their looks turned to horror as one of the two engines appeared to catch fire immediately after the plane had left the ground.

It lost height and ploughed into a two-storey house about 300 yards from the edge of the airfield.

The tail of the plane broke off and burning debris was scattered for about 500 yards around, setting several other houses on fire.

The plane was burned out in the centre section, but the pilot's cockpit seemed to be little damaged.

The captain of the plane was able to scramble free of the wreckage and help in the rescue work before he allowed himself to be taken to hospital.

The B.E.A. issued in London last night the following statement made in Munich by Mr. Anthony Millward, chief executive officer of B.E.A., who had flown out with other officials to the scene of the disaster:

"We are not certain that the aircraft became air-borne but we do know that it overshot the runway and hit a house 300 yards from the end of the runway with its port wing. It then veered to the right, hit a hut and burst into flames.

From The Newcastle Journal Friday 7 February 1958

ASHINGTON PLAYER TELLS IN 2am PHONE CALL OF CRASH ORDEAL

Bobby Charlton: 'I woke to see plane ablaze'

FLUNG OUT 40 YARDS AWAY – 'BUT I'M ALL RIGHT NOW'

IN a telephone talk at 2a.m. today Manchester United's inside-right Bobby Charlton, of Ashington, described his ordeal in the crash.

"The trouble was we did not get off the ground. We taxied, then left the runway, crashed through a fence and hit a house," he told a Reuter correspondent. "The next thing I knew was when I woke up and found myself about 40 yards from the plane, which was blazing violently."

"I had a cut on the head but was otherwise all right. I was a bit scared, though."

He was able to walk, and was one of the first three survivors to get to hospital.

The others were Harry Gregg and Bill Foulkes.

They all helped to get the manager, Matt Busby, into an ambulance.

Worries end

A telegram from Bobby to Ashington Police last night ended hours of worry for his mother, Mrs. Elizabeth Charlton.

Her heart sank when she opened the door to a local policeman – but he smiled as he handed over the telegram from Bobby which said: "I am fit and well. See you all soon."

The telegram ended what Mrs. Charlton described as "The worst day of my life."

She first heard of the crash as she was doing housework at her home in Beatrice Street, Ashington.

A neighbour called. "As soon as I saw his deathly white face I said 'Bobby – the plane' and he nodded," she said last night.

"I did not dare listen to the radio."

"It's a tremendous relief – but those other poor lads," she said sadly.

Also waiting anxiously for news were his younger brothers, Tommy aged 11, and 15-year-old Gordon, a pupil at Bellingham Camp School.

Bobby, who completes National Service in May, is a second cousin of Jackie Milburn.

He was capped for the England schoolboys' team at 15 and was signed by Manchester United when he left Bedlington Grammar School.

From the Ashington Advertiser Friday 18 April 1958

Bobby's mother can handle the Press

The most frequently interviewed woman in Ashington must be 45-year-old Mrs. Elizabeth Charlton, of Beatrice Street, mother of the Manchester United wonder footballer, Bobby Charlton, who at 20 has been capped for England.

As Bobby Charlton moves from triumph to triumph in the football world the newspapermen descend upon housewife Mrs. Charlton to ask what she thinks about her son.

And, of course, she thinks he's wonderful. What mother would not?

Helped Train Him

Reason for the interest of the Press in Mrs. Charlton is that she is known to have perceived Bobby's latent football talent when he was a child, and in encouraging him went so far as to turn out herself into the back streets and the public parks of Ashington to encourage him in kicking a ball around.

When he was an up and coming schoolboy footballer it was noted that he needed a vital quick burst of speed for the breakaway, so Mrs. Charlton helped to select a sprint track in a public park where Bobby, with mother watching him, galloped busily to pull out the extra pace.

Mrs. Charlton herself does not make extravagant claims about her contribution to the making of a star footballer because she says he is "a natural", and that it was always obvious that football would be his business.

At Ease With Press

Now Mrs. Charlton is completely at ease with reporters, because she has been interviewed scores of times. She talks to them freely, but nearly always manages to tell the men on the track of human interest sporting stories that every time she talks to them she has anxieties about what they will print.

Young Tommy

Interesting member of the household is young Tommy, the youngest son, who is still at school, says his game is rugby, and is interested in skiffle.

While mother is being interviewed he sits in a corner fondling a George Formby banjoline and enjoying the limelight his famous brother has brought to his home and life.

Good and Bad

Tailpiece to the Charlton family story concerns a non-member of the clan. This is sport loving newsagent Mr. E. Cockburn who runs a business just along the street from the Charlton home.

In recent weeks it has fallen to his lot to be the bearer of bad tidings and good tidings to the Charlton household. He reluctantly delivered to Mrs. Charlton the first news of the Munich air crash in which Bobby Charlton was one of the lucky ones, then within a week or two more happily was able to deliver the first intimation of young Bobby's award of a place in the England team – his first cap.

Cash and happiness
£20 weekly income
reasonable today,
miners tell T.V.

Money was the main theme of the seven minute spot given to Ashington on the "Tonight" programme which was screened on Monday.

Bearded Fyffe Robertson cross-examined miners and their wives about earnings, the sharing of same between husband and wife, and whether prosperity had given them happiness.

Pit scenes and street scenes appeared fleetingly on the television screen and the interviews introduced local men and women talking in the main about money.

The White House Club figured prominently, with secretary Mr. G. Hall telling millions of viewers about the expenditure of £15,000 on making an old-fashioned miners' club into a luxury meeting place. He talked of sales at the £550 a week level.

"This looks as if there is a good deal of money about in Ashington," commented the B.B.C. reporter with the beard.

*   *   *   *

BETTER OFF

The camera then switched to a couple of men settled in a corner for a quiet drink.

They also were encouraged to talk about money. They said miners as a whole were better off. They agreed that some wages were "pretty high" but "not too high for the cost of living". They talked of wages at the £20 a week level as reasonable for the times, but described the famous £45 a week figure as an isolated and exceptional case with no relation to the general level of earnings.

Asked if more money had brought more happiness, they said there was more happiness because they now had better clothes and television.

"The womenfolk get a lot of things for the home they could not get before, and in the old days they were not happy because they were scraping to make ends meet," one of them declared.

* * * *

They Dare Not

Inevitably a miner was asked the age-old question: "How much do you earn?" The reply was: "I dare not tell you that."

"You don't want your wife to know," suggested the interviewer cheerfully.

The same point cropped up in an interview with a miner in a back street. He was asked why miners always tended to quote low wages, and he replied: "Because he does not want his wife to know."

"I wonder what miners' wives have to say to that?" quipped the bearded interviewer.

The camera then switched to a miner's wife who expressed herself satisfied with the set-up. She was content as long as there was sufficient for the home. As to the rest she was not over curious.

"He likes a drink and a little bit of a gamble, but I have always had sufficient for the home," she explained.

* * * *

Better Than Women

One character, with hands in pockets, bluntly told the world that he never told his wife the amount he earned, claimed that he gave her sufficient money for the home, and that he considered the man was a better saver than the woman.

He gave a shaking to the cosy idea of the heroic thrifty little housewife as the shrewd Chancellor of the Home Exchequer, looking after the feckless husband's money.

Into the breach stepped another miner's wife with a story of a wage of £9 15s. a week to balance the big figures which were being freely bandied about.

She explained that she also went out to work to help pay for a £2,000 house.

The following N.C.B. official average earnings were thrown in by the announcer: Face workers, £18-12-10d.; All underground workers, £17-0-10d.; All workers, £13-6-10d.

And Why Not?

There were brief shots of a well-filled shop, of a well equipped house, and of a back street with one or two parked cars standing about.

And the man with the beard ended the little portrait of Ashington disarmingly with this general comment:

"If miners want to spend some of their money on comfortable clubs why shouldn't they, and if he wants a car why shouldn't he have one?"

From the Ashington Advertiser Friday 26 June 1959

Children enjoy
59th Gala
at Ashington

The 59th Annual Ashington Children's Gala was held last Saturday in the Hirst Welfare Sports Ground. Over 6,600 local children took part and the cash gift of 2/6 was distributed at the entrances, cash being the modern equivalent of the memorable penny, bun, apple, orange and sweets.

Children from Ashington's seven schools marched to the sports ground headed by Lynemouth and Newbiggin Colliery Band, Woodhorn Colliery Band, North Seaton Colliery Band, Ellington Colliery Band and the Salvation Army Band.

In the ground, Woodhorn Band played selections before the commencement of the children's programme, when the various schools gave an exhibition of dancing, a recorder band recital, and a massed singing demonstration.

* * * *

While most parents watched their children competing in the various sports, others examined the exhibition of arts and crafts, by the schoolchildren, which was displayed in Hirst Welfare Gymnasium. The exhibits in the display were of a very high standard, several of them earning high praise from the visiting public. At the close of the exhibition, the cookery exhibits were auctioned.

Among the many well known personalities who attended the Gala was Mr. Will Owen, M.P. who marched down to the Welfare Ground with St. Aidan's schoolchildren, visited the exhibition and then walked round the field watching children competing and chatting to the parents.

The weather was fine, but a blustery wind blew in from the sea, creating flurries of dust which did nothing to dampen the high spirits of the children of Ashington as they were determined to enjoy themselves on this, their particular day.

Prize leek
slashed in
local show

Two 'incidents' marred Ashington's otherwise very smoothly run week-end leek shows when ten were held in Ashington and others at Newbiggin and Lynemouth. Mr. Dick Freeman, of 5, Castle Terrace, Ashington, found that one of his winning leeks at the Linton and Woodhorn show had been slashed while on exhibition. The leek, adjudged the best in the show, was slit in several places with a sharp instrument, the cuts being several inches long. It is thought that a razor blade was used. Several other leeks in the show also received small cuts.

Mr. Freeman, with his brother Harry, have been doing well in recent shows, this week-end they were first and second at the Linton and Woodhorn, and gained a first at the Northern Club next door. As his brother Harry carried away the leeks on Monday morning he said: "It has just been spite on someone's part. The judge said the leek could not have burst, and was good for at least another month. Whoever did it caused minor damage to others to make it look good, but it was my brother's leeks they made sure of."

At Lynemouth, 83 years old Bill Woolage, of 22 Boland Road, entered 18 leeks on Friday evening in the Inn Show, and on Saturday morning nine of them were missing from his garden. He still managed to win third place and a handsome wall stand went with it.

A father and son team won first and second at Hirst East End Club, and incidentally a number of prizes this year showed distinct imagination. There were bathroom weighing machines, hair dryers, carpet cleaning appliances to shampoo your rugs, sets of travelling suitcases, and a coffee table complete with cocktail sets. One show gave a pair of sheets, pillowcases and a wheelbarrow for a prize in the eighties.

Over £3,000 worth of goods were on display at Ashington for the biggest week-end of the leek show season. At the White House Club three colliery managers were among the first twelve prizewinners.

They were Mr. T. L. Smith, manager of Woodhorn Colliery (5th), Mr. J. Dobson, manager of the Duke Pit, and Mr. W. Riches, Ashington Collieries Group manager.

one thing
and   *by Spectator*
ANOTHER

INTO ITS OWN

The leek came into its own with a vengeance last week-end when shows were staged in more than half the clubs of the town. Of course there was the usual bit of bother here and there, when someone or other violently disagreed with the opinion of the judge, and then someone had to have his leeks cut up just to make sure that a particularly good specimen was completely ruined.

I notice that the thousands of people who visit the leek shows don't really go to see the leeks at all. They usually look at the first four or five stands and then have eyes for nothing but the prizes. The womenfolk are particularly more interested in the prizes than in the leeks.

At one club a leek, not a particularly good specimen of the breed, got a prize for having the longest beard – well, that at least provided a little variety.

At another club a prize winner (not very high up), admitted to me that he had never grown a leek in his life and would not be quite certain which end to put in the ground if ever he had to plant them. Still, he managed a 'stand', and was obviously overjoyed with his prize.

STILL ON THE LEEK

You must pardon me harping on about leeks, but on looking through the records of successes over the past few years I have come to the conclusion that there must be one or two families in the town who have more kitchen cabinets, cocktail cabinets, sets of bedding and so forth in their homes than they know what to do with. Such are the rewards of being able to grow good leeks, and I probably am more than a little jealous of their achievements in this field.

Without knowing the first or last thing about leeks, I thought the best two stands were at the White House Social Club – they looked as if they would have held a very high place in any show.

From the Advertiser Friday 23 October 1964

The "Black Monk" gets around fast

Is it mass hallucination or young people's imagination? Whoever the 'Black Monk' is he must have transport – supernatural or petrol driven. Reports from schoolchildren of all ages, from infant to grammar school, all tally about the 'Black Monk', allegedly seen at Ashington, Blyth, North Seaton and Newcastle.

Parents of Ashington schoolchildren were all told the same tale by their offspring last week, with some embellishments.

A tall hooded figure, with cloak, in black, had been seen in the Hirst area, they alleged. Some have seen him carrying a shining axe, while others are reported to have seen him carrying a curved hook.

One girl was said to have been scratched on the face by the mysterious figure.

Even grammar school pupils from Newcastle report the same story, again with added dressings.

But Ashington police report that they have not received any complaints about the Black Monk. They know about the story, having children of their own, who reported the same tales.

"We have not received any complaints about this mystery man, but we are keeping a watch on the situation," said an Ashington police spokesman at the weekend.

As the stories spread, children have added their own local flavour to the 'tale from school'.

Fish hooks scratched a girl's face, one story went; the figure disappears when a policeman is about; it becomes invisible and passes through walls; the black-cowled thing has staring eyes; the axe it carries has a blade of shining steel; it sometimes appears out of nowhere.

Two Blyth girls allege they have seen the figure, but young imaginations, coupled with darkening nights, can turn a tree into a wrinkled armed monster.

Another theory advanced is that schoolchildren start on projects of local history at this time of year, and old tales of haunted priories become a little too real to them.

Hallowe'en is also not very far away, and horror films are quite common today.

The only thing that is puzzling, is how the same tale was heard in two separate areas, 20 miles apart, on the same day?

Other books from Zymurgy

Natural North
by Allan Potts
Foreword by the Duke of Northumberland

A photographic celebration of flora and fauna in the North of England. Supporting text provides background information. Sections cover; high fells, upland, woodland, agricultural, coastal and urban areas.

ISBN 1 903506 00X hb 160pp £16.99

Bent Not Broken
by Lauren Roche

Lauren Roche's autobiography; an abused child, stowaway, stripper, prostitute, drug abuser. She turned her life around to become a doctor. An international best seller. Lauren has been interviewed by Lorraine Kelly, Esther Rantzen, Johnny Walker, Simon Mayo and others.

ISBN 1 903506 026 pb 272pp + 8pp plate section £6.99

A Lang Way To The Pawnshop
by Thomas Callaghan
Introduction by Sid Chaplin

An autobiographical account of growing up in 1930s urban Britain; a family of ten, two bedrooms, no wage earner. An amusing insight into a period of history still in living memory.

ISBN 1 903506 018 pb 144pp £6.99

The Krays: The Geordie Connection
by Steve Wraith and Stuart Wheatman
Foreword by Dave Courtney

After seeing the Krays at a funeral on the news (aged ten) Steve writes letters, meets the brothers and eventually becomes one of 'the chaps'. The book is about the Krays final years and how they ran things on the outside.

ISBN 1 903506 042 pb 240pp + 8pp plate section£6.99

The River Tyne From Sea to Source
by Ron Thornton
Foreword by Robson Green

A collection of nearly eighty water colours and hundreds of pencil drawings following the River Tyne from outside the harbour to the source of the North and South Tyne rivers. Supporting text provides a wealth of information on the history surrounding the Tyne.

ISBN 1 903506 034 hb 160pp £16.99

Life On The Line
by Lauren Roche

Following on from Bent Not Broken the book covers Lauren's life once she becomes a doctor. Bankruptcy, depression, a suicide attempt - and the shock revelation that her son was a sex offender. What can a mother do when she suspects that one of her children is being abused? What happens when you discover that the abused child has become an abuser?

ISBN 1 903506 050 pb 192pp + 8pp plate section £6.99

A Memoir of The Spanish Civil War
by George Wheeler
Foreword by Jack Jones
Edited by David Leach

Thousands from across the world went to Spain to form the International Brigades; many did not return. Through George Wheeler's experience and memories of the Spanish Civil War you will discover what the war was really like. What were they fighing for? Why did the Spanish people fail in their fight against facism?
    1 903506 077 pb 192pp + 8pp plate section £8.99

Alcatraz Island Memoirs of a Rock Doc
by Milton Daniel Beacher, M.D
Edited by Dianne Beacher Perfit

MiltonDaniel Beacher, M.D. arrived on Alcatraz Island a naive and compassionate young doctor. One year later he left with a journal.It chronicled the suicides, discipline problems, force feedings , and details of a long strike and successful escape.

He also penned conversations with famous prisoners like Al Capone, Alvin Karpis and Machine Gun Kelly. Dr Beacher later worve the journal into a vivid acoount of life on the Rock.
    1 903506 085 pb240 pp + 8pp plate section £6.99

Back Lanes and Muddy Pitches
by Robert Rowell

A book about playing football and growing up. Robert Rowell's football career starts within earshot and eyesight of mum; with lamp posts for floodlights and garage doors for goals. When he gets older matches are played in the park with jumpers for goalposts. Robert gets the ultimate call-up, a place in the school team. After leaving school, student life, then the joys of starting work. The book follows Robert's life through football to middle–age.

A book for everyone who enjoys football and reading.

1 9103506 12 3 pb 288 pp £6.99

Soapy Business
Through The Mangle
by John Solomon

Set in the 1950s in the days before supermarkets and identikit town centres. John reveals the cut–and–thrust world of the soap salesman – with on–going tussles with grocers and devious methods of beating his competitors. 'Suds Law' if things could go wrong, they often did. John travelled the north east in his daily battle with eccentric grocers.

A charming and light hearted read, full of warmth and optimism.

1 903506 14 X pb 178 pp £7.99

Willi Whizkas
– Tall Tales and Lost Lives!
by Paws and Claws

Willi Whizkas is an ordinary cat who shares his home with two humans. He is fed up with the same cat food every day, envious of his friends – they all have cat flaps and he hates the vet.

His life is far from humdrum and routine. He has a great set of friends, loves exploring and having adventures.

A must read for all cat lovers.

1 903506 18 2 pb 256 pp £7.99

Northstars
by Sid Smith, Chris Phipps and John Tobler

A celebration of musicians with north–eastern roots, based on exclusive interviews from Royal Television Society award winning TyneTees series of the same name. The book honours the role of north–east musicians in the history of popular music.

From rock 'n' roll to heavy rock, pop to punk, electonic to acoustic folk, Northstars documents how musicians from the region have made it to the world stage.

1903506 09 3 pb 256pp £12.99

Rats, Bat and Strange Toilets
– Travel Tips for Unusual Countries
by David Freemantle

An entertaining travel book with serious undertones. It offers a range of useful and occasionally useless tips, insights and advice for travellers.

Featured on BBC Radio 4 Excess Baggage and in The Times Travel Supplement.

1903506 21 1 pb 240pp £7.99

548
135
423
1001